DEADLY DESIRES

ASHLEY MCKNIGHT

Editing: Dot The i Edit
Cover Design: Disturbed Valkyrie Designs
Formatting: Disturbed Valkyrie Designs

This is considered a dark, contemporary romance and delves into heavy topics such as on page SA, body shaming, and self harm that some readers may find disturbing and/or triggering. Please read at your own discretion. Your mental health matters.

This book is intended for 18+, mature audiences.

For those who've overcome past trauma and still get railed into dawn... this one's for you.

Prologue

Melody

Nine months ago

The rain pitter patters on the shingles of my house, a song desperate with longing for the sun. The wind is howling, screaming its defiance to any that will listen...

I'm listening. It's all I can do. All I've become is a shell of myself since that night. A night so twisted, I revisit it in my nightmares each time I go to sleep. The medication barely works, but my doctor won't up the prescription. Sleep evades me like the moon evades the sun. A clap of thunder shakes the house and I startle. Loud noises launch me into panic attacks that steal my breath and cloud my vision. This storm is raging a battle against me, but inside, I'm too numb to care to even arm myself to fight back.

Most nights I lie awake contemplating life and how to end it. I am a survivor, but I have no idea how much longer I can claim that title. Most days I fight the need to cut, to release this energy within my soul lest it burst out of my very being in ways that would hurt those around me. I wear the scars of my failed battles on my wrists, hidden behind long sweaters and jackets that I can always be found in. I long for peace, to be rid of this constant, all consuming pain.

I am broken.

My parents say it about me in hushed tones they don't think I can hear at the lavish parties and charity events they host. I suppose I am, though I have no energy to care or dispel their belief. They tell me I need to get out more, go hang out with my friends, or meet a new guy. But they don't understand. They don't understand I physically, mentally, and emotionally have no energy for any of it. I barely have enough energy to paste on a smile at the events and hold myself tall with poise and grace as I make idle small talk with old Mrs. Anderson, one of our charity sponsors who is always decked out in massive amounts of diamonds.

This is depression, anxiety, and PTSD wrapped into one shell of a person.

I dream of better days, where I am whole and well. It seems like such a foreign notion. I think back to who I was a year ago; a bright college student going for her bachelor's degree in criminal law and the star linemen on the college football team was proposing to her during their championship win. Life was good. Until it wasn't only three months ago. Until life shattered everything I thought I knew and hoped to be. I dropped out of college. I couldn't handle it at all with my depression, suffering from anxiety attacks anytime someone got too close to me, or even bumped into me. My parents knew what happened, and my friends suspected, but I'll keep that secret until I'm dead and cold inside.

Other than my parents, there is only one other that knows my secret... and that was my then-fiancé, Brian. Although he claimed he wanted to spend the rest of his life with me, that all changed once he found out what happened that fateful night. How broken I am inside. I would be a stain on his otherwise pristine reputation, and he didn't want to risk his career with my "drama." We both run in the same upper class; there is no room to be dragged down by me. He ended things immediately, wanting no part in who I now am. I quickly learned that it was best not to utter a single word to anyone else. Because surely they would do the same —cut me from their lives and abandon me. So instead, I've pushed everyone away so they can't hurt me first.

ONE

MELODY

PRESENT DAY

Today I am going out job searching... *blehhhh*. What money I had saved up in my account, and have been surviving on for the last year, has started to dwindle. I realize I can't keep surviving on ramen noodles and my parents. While I have my associate's degree in criminal law, I want to find something that I love doing. Don't get me wrong... I do want to return to law someday, I just can't bring myself to be faced with horrors much like my own right now. I prefer to find a job that keeps me as far away from those troubles as possible. Plus, my therapist agrees with me, so it must be the right choice.

Walking down Main Street, I keep a close eye on each store I pass in hopes of seeing a hiring sign. Before I know it, I come across my favorite store and can't resist making a stop. As I pause outside our city's little bookstore, a sign catches my eye in the window. *Now Hiring* in bold red letters that scream desperation. *Could this really be happening?!* It must seriously be my lucky day.

Making my way into the store, I feel at peace for once. Books hold my heart in a way no man ever could. I feel a weight lifted from my shoulders as I take in the cozy room. The morning sunlight streams into the room from large bay windows that are accompanied by a plush couch and chair for customers that want to do a little reading. There are built in bookshelves that line each wall, and in the open space there are numerous little tables holding a variety of books, most labeled by a small sign for which genre they fall into. I beeline straight for the TikTok spicy section. Although I have very little, if none at all in my life currently, romance has always been my favorite genre when it comes to books, and this little store specializes in all things romance.

After browsing for a bit, and reading the back of a few books, I make my selection and head to the register. A young girl, maybe in her early twenties, with blonde hair pulled back in a ponytail, bright blue eyes, a dusting of freckles, and a name tag that says "Brooke," waits at a large mahogany counter ready to check me out. She seems so warm and welcoming that I immediately feel at ease.

"Hello," I say with a small smile as I lay my single book on the counter.

"Hey! Did you find everything OK?"

"Yes, thanks. I saw you have a *Now Hiring* sign in the window. I was wondering if I could apply?" I ask, hope brimming to the top.

I think her eyes might bulge out of her head with the excitement radiating from her very being.

"O.M.G., you absolutely can! When can you start?"

"Umm... don't I need to fill out an application?"

"I'm actually the owner. I have a good feeling about you based on your book selection alone!" She winks and I blush. "No need for all that nonsense. By the way, my name's Brooke."

"Melody. Nice to meet you," I reply.

We shake hands and exchange phone numbers. Even though I am caught off guard, I ask her a few more questions about the job and the hours. I'd be working 11 A.M. to 5 P.M. every day, plus Saturdays from 9 A.M. to 3 P.M.

It's not forty hours like I was hoping to find, but it's close enough, and I'll take whatever I can get right now. And surprisingly, the pay is pretty good, actually really damn good for a little bookshop on Main Street.

Anything that helps me to stop living off money from my parents. Plus, I love books; what else could I possibly ask for? Brooke also seems very nice, and a typical young adult with all the exuberance and excitement of a young teen. I accept the job and Brooke states that I can start tomorrow at 8 A.M., a little early, so she can train me on the basics before the store opens. I've never been a morning person but at least it's only one early day a week.

I thank her for the opportunity and leave the store, clutching my book to my chest and a small smile on my face. Maybe life is taking a turn for the better. Maybe, just maybe, I can find that spark for life again.

08:45

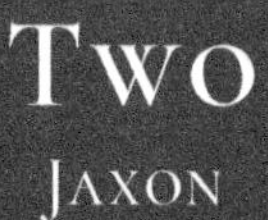

Two

Jaxon

She doesn't see me as she leaves my little sister's bookshop, almost bumping into me as she goes.

"Excuse me, sorry." She rushes out as she scrambles not to drop her coffee and the book in her arms. She doesn't even glance my way as she fumbles with her things. She's skittish and ready to take flight, much like a little bird.

I've been watching her since I caught sight of her walking down the street earlier this morning. She's beautiful. She wears little to no makeup, but she doesn't need it. She has skin like porcelain, all smooth and unblemished other than a few piercings that accentuate her face. She has long brown hair pulled back into a messy bun, eyes as green as springtime grass, and curves that make me want to bite my fist. She definitely has some extra cushion; her plump ass and generous breasts are apparent even under the coat she wears. And do I ever have a thing for voluptuous women.

She's average height, maybe five foot six inches, but definitely considered short when compared to my towering six foot five inch frame. I am instantly transfixed by her. I don't know why that is, especially seeing that I have no shortage of women to choose from, but suddenly they all pale in comparison to her. None of them transfix me the way she does.

She hurries off, leaving me looking after her as she goes. I guess I'll stop and say hi to little sister later. I follow but not too closely. I mix in with the crowd on main street, never losing sight of her cute, messy bun. When she left the bookstore, I noticed dark circles under her eyes like she doesn't get much sleep. It triggers something in me. She walks with a slight skip to her step now, making me instantly angry that I am not the source of that happiness. This is absurd. I don't even know this woman, and I'm already obsessed with wanting her. *How is she doing this to me?*

I continue walking after her, even as she turns the corner and gets in her car. *It appears she parked conveniently close to me.* As I walk a little further down the road and past her vehicle, I do a quick peek behind me, relieved to see she's still sitting in her car. The car that looks like she probably comes from money, although, I can't see the make and model from where I am, just that it's black and sleek. I get in my car and buckle up as soon as I see her put on the blinker. I can't have her driving away before I get a chance to see where my mystery woman lives.

As she peels off into traffic, I wait a few cars behind before pulling out with my BMW M8 F92. She's an alpine white beauty but is mainly the vehicle I take to and from work. I have a few other vehicles, but this one is the most inconspicuous for when I go out around the town, and definitely the least expensive compared to my others. As I watch from afar, I memorize her license plate for when I get home and can give it to Franklin, the greatest hacker south of Silicon Valley. He's the best of the best, my closest friend, and one of the few people I actually trust. He'll be able to dig up everything I need to know about my little sparrow.

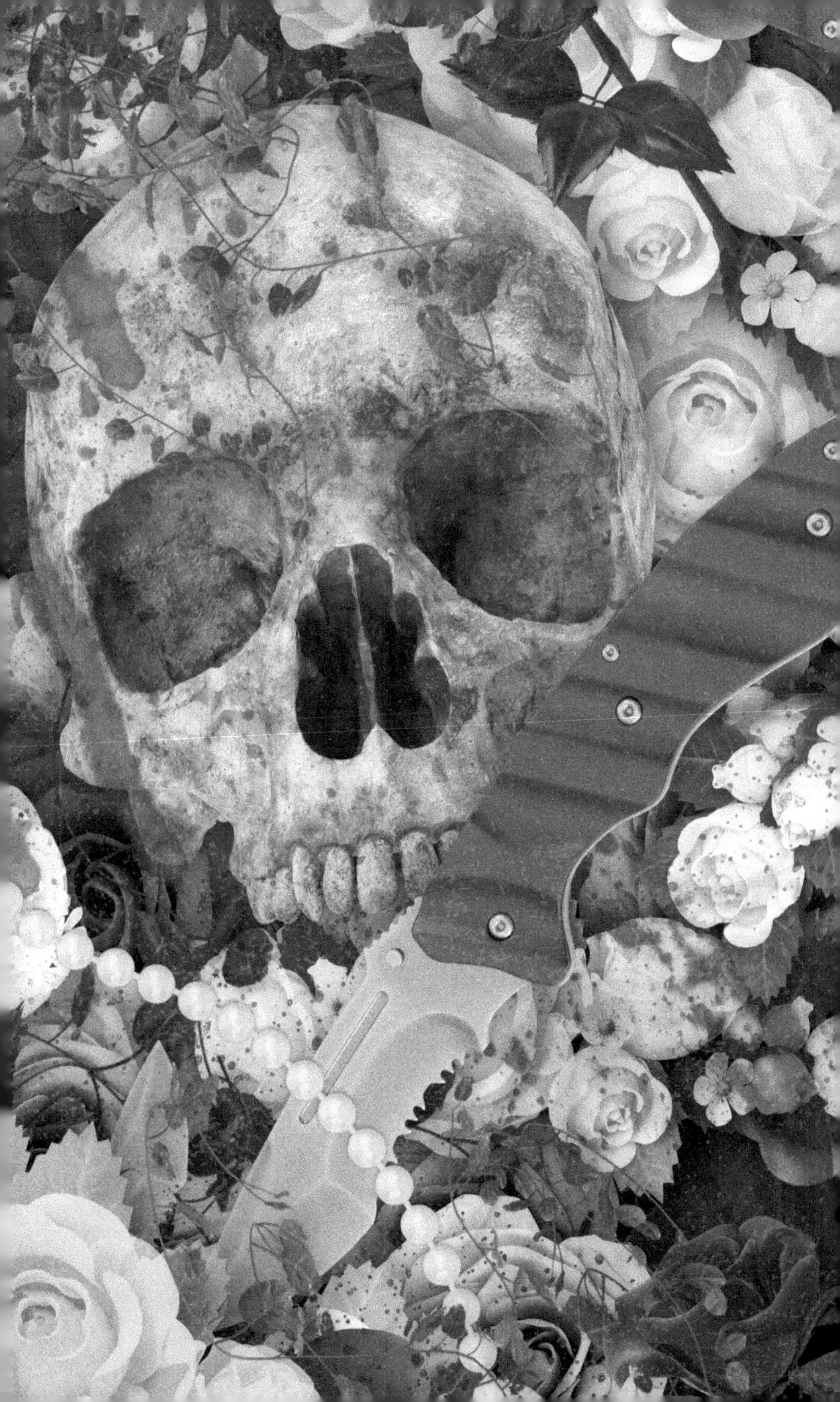

THREE

MELODY

It's way too early for this. I set my alarm for 6 A.M., but I hit snooze one too many times so now I'm running behind schedule. I'm nervous, but I have a good feeling about this job. Brooke just seems so nice and I'm looking forward to working someplace where I have some independence.

All the other jobs I've ever had, I always had someone breathing down my neck to make sure I did my job right. But here, I have freedom. The pay is phenomenal and being surrounded by books is another plus.

Once I'm all ready, my makeup lightly done, I leave the house realizing that I have no time to stop at the little coffee shop next to my new job. Oh well, guess I have to power through the day. I get in my car, blast some music, and make my way into town.

I show up a few minutes early, thank god—a habit I picked up from my mom. *It's better to be early than late*, she always used to say, and it's been instilled in me ever since.

I walk through the door to One More Chapter and find Brooke with a sage colored cart full of books. The morning sun is casting light within the store, creating a feeling of nostalgia and bliss. The sweet aroma of coffee is in the air, and I instantly regret not waking up earlier to get my coffee fix.

"Hey girl! I'm so glad you made it! There's a coffee machine behind the counter and creamer in the mini fridge if you want to help yourself before we get started," she says excitedly.

"Oh my god, thank you. I woke up late today and didn't have time to stop. You're a lifesaver!"

"No problem! Feel free to help yourself to coffee or water in the fridge during your shifts too. I buy it specifically for us. Can't be surviving without coffee these days!"

"Isn't that the truth. Thank you again, I truly appreciate it."

"Once you're done getting your coffee, come over by me and I'll show you the ropes on stocking the books and displays."

We spend the next hour going through how to scan the books and categorize them throughout the store. I'm also shown how to stock the merchandise. They have everything from coffee mugs, candles, bookmarks, stickers, tote bags, and even vibrators by the spicy section of the store.

She shows me the storage room where all the books and merchandise are kept. It'll be my responsibility to keep the store stocked during my shifts, but other than that, the job itself seems easy enough. Brooke even let me know during slow periods, if all tasks are done and caught up on, I can bring a book to read during my shift; preferably a book in the store so I have recommendations for customers that ask for them. I don't know how this job could get any better, but I am completely sold!

Brooke has to be the sweetest boss I've ever had. Even though she's younger than me, she seems like an old soul. I've learned quite a bit about her from our morning learning the ropes. Brooke majored in English and is twenty-three years old. Her and her brother were adopted by their aunt and uncle when they were little and lost their parents to a car accident. She opened the bookstore immediately after college and never looked back. She's the youngest of her siblings. Apparently, her aunt and uncle also took in two other boys, both older than her. Brooke also mentioned that her biological brother was a significant help to getting the bookshop up and running, helping her fund the opening inventory order and completely renovating the space to what it is now.

"So tell me a little more about you, girl," she queries.

"Not much to tell other than I'm an only child from a wealthy family. I'm twenty-eight years old. My parents have raised me to present myself by their standards, so you can imagine how upset they were when I got my piercings and tattoos. I ruined their perfect little princess," I reply, sarcasm dripping from my last sentence and a chuckle slipping past my lips.

"I was once pursuing a degree in criminal law, but I haven't worked in the field in over a year now. I wanted to find something I loved doing. It upsets my parents that I'm not going back into law, but oh well." I shrug my shoulders while taking a sip of my coffee.

"Sounds like you were raised with some pretty high standards. Any love interest in your life?" she asks while waggling her eyebrows.

"HA, definitely not. I am A-OK being single. I was engaged at one point, but that's a story for another time."

"WOW! I can't wait to hear that one. Guy must have been quite the douche to let you go."

"Something like that," I reply.

"You should get back out there! Date around a bit!" she suggests.

"I've thought about it... but I don't even know if I know how to flirt anymore, it's been so long since I dated anyone."

"Well, you never know until you try. I'm sure it's like riding a bike," she says slyly with a wink.

"True... maybe I'll give it a chance... we'll see," I hesitantly reply. I'm not ready to dive into this conversation, and I think she gets the hint, because next thing you know she's switching the topic back to the store.

"So, what made you want to work here of all places then?"

"My love for books. Specifically, romance. I was desperate for a job too. It just worked out that I saw the hiring sign in your window, like divine intervention."

"I totally believe in that stuff! I think it was definitely fate. We are going to be best friends! Just you watch!"

I'm a little caught off guard by her statement as it's only my first day, but Brooke has such an infectious personality. I would be lying if I said I couldn't see us being fast friends. I just hope that I can be a good enough friend. I've spent so long pushing people away, I don't know if I can be what people need... what people want.

AFTER MY SHIFT IS OVER, I HEAD STRAIGHT HOME. Brooke's words from earlier in the day resonate in my mind. *Maybe I should open up my Tinder and just see what's out there.* As I heat up my leftover spaghetti and pour myself a generous glass of wine, I re-download Tinder from the Cloud. I haven't used it since before Brian and I started dating... it's been so long.

My phone pings, signaling the download has completed; I grab my spaghetti and wine, my comfy blanket, and curl up on the couch. As I eat, I log into my Tinder and start scrolling. After realizing that I have to pay to see my likes and actually message people, I get up to get my wallet.

As I pass my front windows, something catches my eye in my peripheral vision, but when I look over, it's gone. *I am really starting to lose it...* I could have sworn I saw a person across the street, staring at my house. I get a wave of the chills. I shake it off and grab my wallet. I swing by the front door on my way to make sure it's locked and the deadbolt is activated before doing the same for the back door.

Never can be too safe.

Once I have Tinder paid for, I start scrolling. Some of these men make me almost snort out my wine. I'm swiping left far more than I am swiping right. I can't help but start to feel discouraged. *Maybe I shouldn't have done this...* I get up quickly and pour myself another glass of wine. Sweet red wine, or any dessert wine really, is my favorite drink in the evenings to unwind. Satisfied with my over generous pour, I head back to the couch and continue swiping and viewing profiles. Seriously, some of these men are just audacious in their pursuit of a female body to warm their bed.

As the wine loosens me up, I can't help the giggles that are slipping past my otherwise cool and collected exterior. Figuring it's getting late, I go through a few more swipes for the night. Going back to review all the men I swiped right on, I find the folder empty. *What the heck?!* The app must have a bug.

Before I throw my phone down on the couch with frustration, I exit the app, force close it, and open it back up. *Maybe that'll reset it or something.* The first person to populate on my feed has my mouth popping open with a silent *woooooow*. He has short-cut, black hair, a short beard that appears well kept and trimmed, light blue almost silver eyes, and pierced ears. I'm assuming he's also covered in tattoos by the few that are inked on his neck peeking from his shirt. The man is mouth watering—a straight up Adonis.

Now that the picture has intrigued me, I click on it to view his profile. I'm not too surprised by what I find first; he loves motorcycles and sports cars. I could have easily pegged him for that type by his looks alone. I keep scrolling to look at his details. What I *am* surprised by is that he labeled himself as a Potterhead. I'm impressed. Those books made me discover my love for reading. His name is Jaxon, he's twenty-nine-years-old—only one year older than me—and is looking for a monogamous relationship. *Hmm*, not sure if I'm ready for a full-on relationship though.

Going out on a limb, I decide to scroll up and officially swipe right on him. It's a long shot with him being so gorgeous and me being... well, me. I swirl my wine and take another sip.

Before I can even set my wine down, I see an alert light up my phone screen with a notification that I've been matched. Nervousness blossoms in my stomach, but it's quickly replaced by a liquid courage burning it away with each sip of my wine. I open the app and go to my notifications. I click on the match alert and almost drop my wine.

What are the chances? No, seriously. What are the chances that it's the hottie that is tatted and pierced? *Is it a full moon tonight?* I'm spiraling. This can't be happening. Any liquid courage I had is officially gone. I'm definitely not even in his league. You would think someone like him should be with a skinny blonde with perky tits who has an equal love for fast vehicles.

Thinking it's probably a mistake, I exit Tinder and hold down my finger on the app icon. The options quickly display, and I immediately click "delete app". I'm hyperventilating, my anxiety is through the roof.

I can't do this.

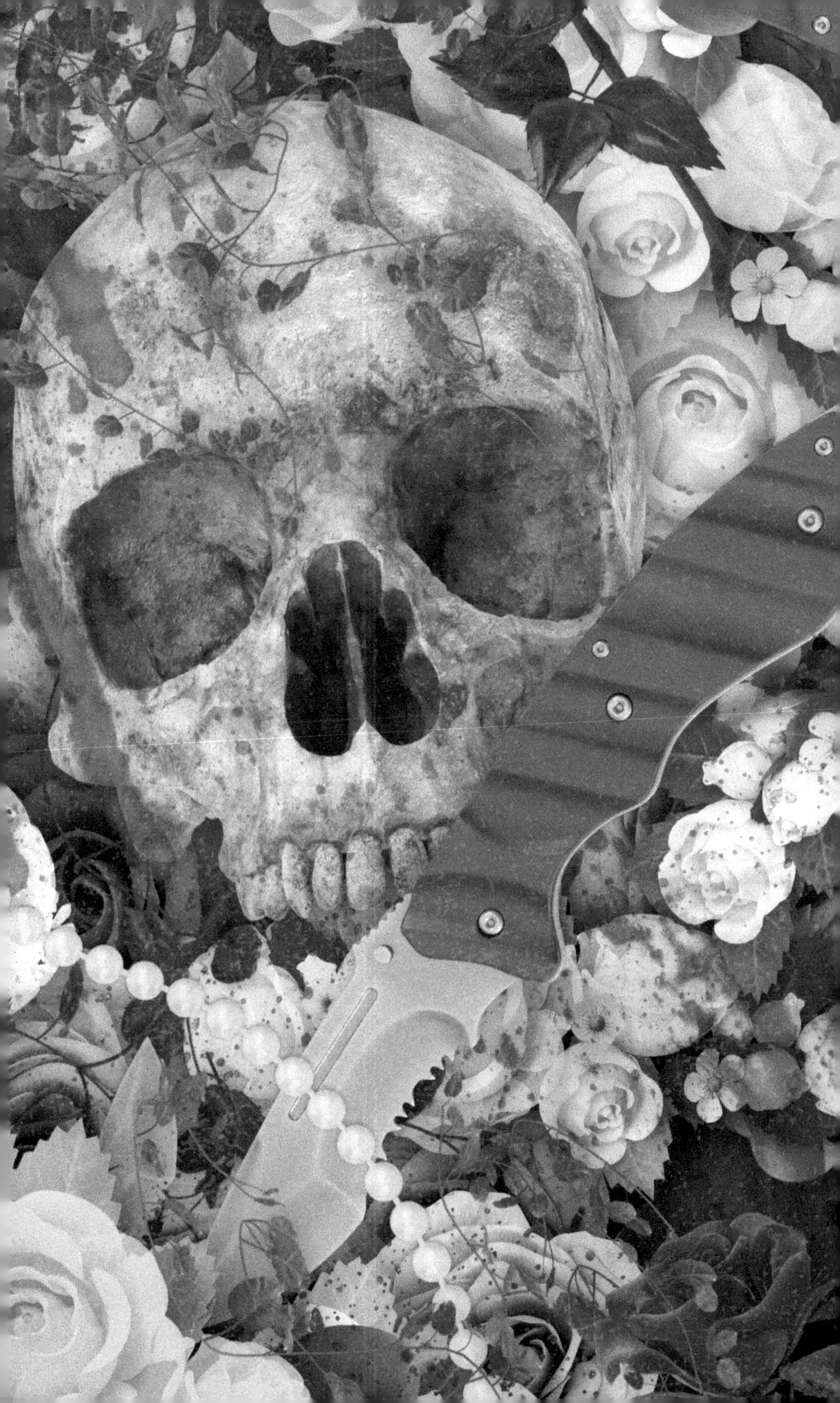

Chapter 3.5

Unknown

So my sweet song is finally coming back out into the world. No more hiding away at home, no more hiding away from me.

I noticed another man following her yesterday. He piqued my interest enough that the big bad monster has decided he wants to come out and play, and claim what is rightfully his.

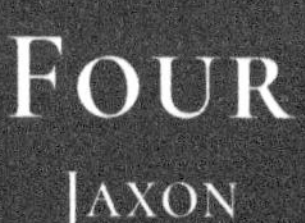

FOUR

JAXON

I stopped by her place tonight, hoping to catch a glimpse of my little sparrow. Pulling up to her street, I cut the lights to my BMW so I didn't bring any unwanted attention to myself and parked down the street. The night was quiet and the street dimly light; all the better for checking in on her.

She lives in a nice house, which makes me wonder what she does for a living. The house is a crisp white with a black metal roof and a two-car, attached garage. If I had to guess by the size it probably has two or three bedrooms. The house is definitely a modern farmhouse type, which seems to be all the rage right now. On the left side of the house is a large bay window, where I can see her cozied up with a blanket on the couch. Why she leaves her curtains open for just anyone to watch her is causing my jaw to tick in frustration.

Once I saw her get up from the couch, I slithered back into the shadows and made my way back to my vehicle. My little sparrow is safe at home, and that's all that matters.

On my way to Franklin's house, I pick up a pizza from Bonetti's Pizzeria and some beers for Franklin, as well as a bottle of Macallan for myself. Franklin loves his pineapple teriyaki pizza. I personally can't stand pineapple on pizza, but I owe him for doing me another favor.

Franklin is always quick to respond to my requests, even if he's currently playing one of those video games he loves so much; he always makes time for me. As I suspected, he didn't disappoint. I immediately gave him her information when I was on my way back home last night, and boy has he delivered.

After parking my car in his driveway, I make my way up to his house, food and drinks in hand. He lives modestly even though he has no shortage of money; his business brings in good money. From the front window, I can see lights flashing. Probably playing one of his shooter games. Finding the front door unlocked, per usual, I walk into the house and yell over the sounds of machine guns and bombs to announce my arrival.

"Hey, Franklin! I got the goods, man."

Franklin says something into his mic and backs out of his game. Turning off the console, he looks over at me and says smugly, "So do I."

He hands me a folder and I get to work going through everything. Once I finish going through the information in the folder, I make my way through the bits that he has pulled up on his laptop. The whole process takes me nearly an hour and a half.

Franklin found everything from her name, which is Melody Ann Harper, to her social security number. He found where she went to school, her jobs, her tax documents, and he was even able to hack into her iPad that she keeps at home and her cellphone. He pulled up her complete records from high school through college. My little sparrow was quite the student; straight A's in all her classes and she participated in numerous extra curricular activities. All of this, just from her license plate number and address. I'm impressed.

He also managed to hack into her Facebook and Instagram accounts. I thoroughly enjoyed going through those. From what I could gather across her platforms is that she was previously engaged to a guy named Brian... I want to punch his face. The fact that he had my little sparrow in his grasp for any amount of time makes my very being simmer with barely contained rage. Based on her message history, it didn't end well with him. Somehow she slipped from his grasp. *All the better for me anyway.*

What I found to be most intriguing was the fact that Franklin also stumbled upon her dating profile on Tinder. Apparently, she's had it for years but a new login was pinged about thirty minutes ago. *What are you up to, little sparrow?*

"Dude, you should make a profile real quick," says Franklin, breaking the silence as we both read over all the information.

"Can you get us matched up," I ask, feeling optimistic at this turn of events.

"What do I look like, some magical wizard?" At his sarcasm, I level him with a glare.

"Just kidding, Jax, of course I can."

I quickly create and pay for an account, customize all my details, and upload a few pictures.

"Done. Work your magic."

I hand over my phone and Franklin turns to his monitors and gets to work. I'm not too savvy with his technology so I sit back on the couch and wait for him to finish up. I can't sit still though so I start to pace, running my hands through my hair nervously.

I see Franklin peek over at me while he works. He's probably wondering what's come over me. He's never seen me like this over a woman before. Most women are in my bed for the night and gone the next. Before I can ask what's taking so long, he hands me back my phone.

"Alright, Jax, you're all set to go. I have the two of you matched up. I also deleted the other guys she swiped right on. Now, let's give her time and see if she reaches out or if you have to make the first move."

I nearly growl at the possessiveness that comes over me. *Melody.* Of course I will be reaching out first. I can't wait for some other guy to try to sweep her off her feet or try to use her for a quick fuck. *She's mine. All. Fucking. Mine.* From the moment I spotted her walking down the street, she belonged to me. Now... I just need to get my little sparrow's attention.

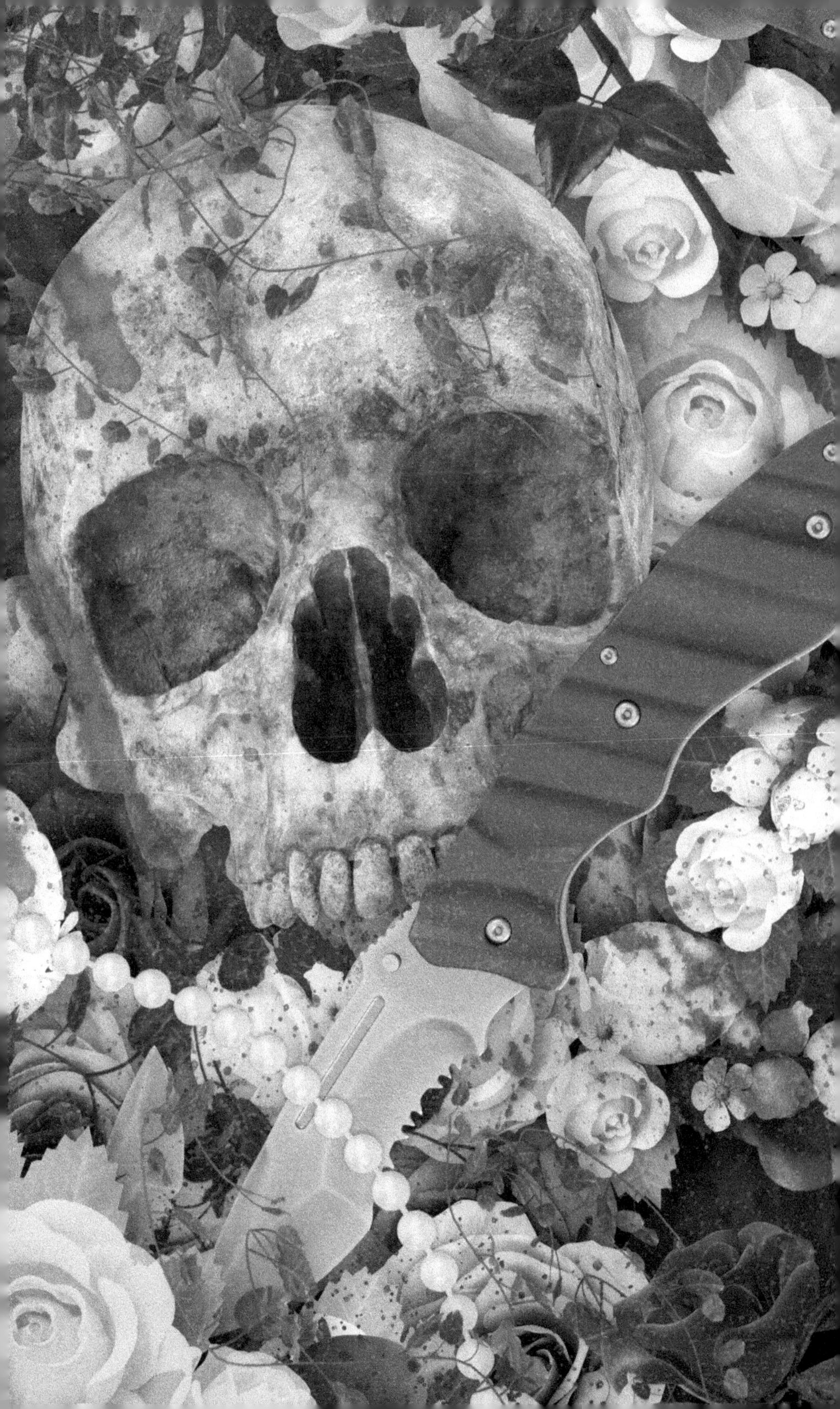

FIVE

MELODY

I'm woken the next day by the sunlight streaming in through my bedroom window. I must have forgotten to close my blackout curtains. Groaning, I reach over, tug them shut, and close my eyes. I try for what feels like an hour to fall back asleep, but it's no use. I'm up. I glance at the clock on my bedside table. 8:17 A.M. Sundays I normally sleep in 'til at least 11 A.M., but here I am, wide awake and remembering the events of last night.

I still can't believe I matched with probably the hottest guy on that damn app. Throwing an arm over my eyes, I'm feeling embarrassed that I even swiped right. I was probably a joke to him. Ughhh, but he was so hot. He had enough muscles that it probably wouldn't take much for him to throw me around. *OH MY GOD.* I really need to stop... or get laid. Probably just stop while I'm ahead, but I can't help when my eyes dart over to my nightstand. I don't remember the last time I had an orgasm.

Sighing, I reach over and grab my rose vibrator from the drawer. Since I take antidepressants, reaching climax has always been an issue, but I swear by the rose. It has been a literal sex-life saver.

Turning the device on, I leave it in idle mode while I slip my hand under my shirt. My stomach is soft without any hint of muscle. I continue my slow perusal and make my way to my right breast. I start to imagine Jaxon. My cheeks flare with embarrassment but I push it down. He'll never know.

I flick my nipple and imagine his teeth biting me, enough to cause pain but not enough that I don't enjoy it. My back arches, pushing my breasts against my shirt. I roll my nipple before making my way over to my other breast, giving it the same attention I did to its twin. My other hand reaches up and clasps my throat, applying slight pressure to the sides. I let go just as my vision starts to fade around the edges, getting off on the pain and loss of blood to my brain.

I imagine Jaxon kissing his way down my body, not at all repulsed by my curves and softness. I trail my fingers lightly between my inner thighs before reaching the edge of my panties. I cup myself and can already feel how wet I am. I grind my palm on my sensitive clit and buck my hips.

Grabbing my rose, I turn it to the slowest setting before placing it under my panties to the place I'm most sensitive. The sensation is immediate. I'm moaning out and clicking the button to a faster speed. It's no longer the rose, but Jaxon's mouth on my clit, sucking and licking like a starved man. My legs fall open and my other hand goes back to my breast. I'm pinching and rolling my nipple at the same time as my clit is being sucked and tugged. I up the speed again and just as I pinch my nipple, I come undone, and it's Jaxon's name I'm moaning out with my release.

God, it feels so good that I don't remove the vibrator. Instead, I quickly get built up for a second orgasm. I'm heaving, shutting my eyes, and imagining Jaxon throwing my legs over his shoulders before he lines up with my center. I fall over the edge again, this time shouting out repeatedly while my hips lift and I ride the sensation out for as long as I can.

It's a really good thing I don't live in my parent's home anymore. I turn off the rose and set it on the nightstand as I lay back and try to catch my breath. That had to be one of the best double orgasms I've given myself in a while. I couldn't help but imagine Jaxon working himself on my body. That man is sin. I bet all the ladies probably do what I did—imagine Jaxon worshiping their bodies and giving themselves the best orgasms of their life. I'm halfway tempted to redownload the app and message him, but I think better of it.

I get up and make my way to my en suite bathroom where I wash my hands and my vibrator with special cleaner. I take a good look in the mirror. There is a flush to my face that hints at being freshly fucked. I peer at myself through my lashes as I hang my head down, arms braced on the sink. I'm definitely a curvy girl, with a soft belly, breasts that would surely spill over a man's large hands, and thighs that rub together, even when I spread my feet shoulder width apart. My thighs and ass are dimpled with fat, which I usually smooth out with shape-wear. I have piercing green eyes that are actually my favorite feature because they have an inner circle of gold. I'm a brunette with full wavy hair, streaked with lowlights and highlights. Most days I do messy buns because I just have no energy to do anything else with it. I don't look horrible, but I imagine a man like Jaxon likes his women with toned stomachs and asses and perky tits. I definitely don't check any of those boxes.

Pushing off of the sink, I make my way back into the bedroom to my walk-in closet to grab fresh clothes. Given it's a Sunday, I'm not getting dressy. Some gray sweat pants, black sneakers, and an oversized sweater will do just fine. I head back to the bathroom, set my clothes on the counter, and start up the shower. The room quickly fills with steam and I get in, washing away all hints of my escapade in the bedroom.

Toweling off after my shower, I quickly get dressed and go downstairs to make a coffee. Sundays are the best days to explore the downtown area and stop at the library. I used to love doing a little retail therapy and then taking my books to read at the park.

Mom and Dad won't care that I use my card linked to the family bank account a while longer. Actually, they would probably be happy to hear about me going out in the world. There is something so calming about all of these activities; they are a perfect way to end my week.

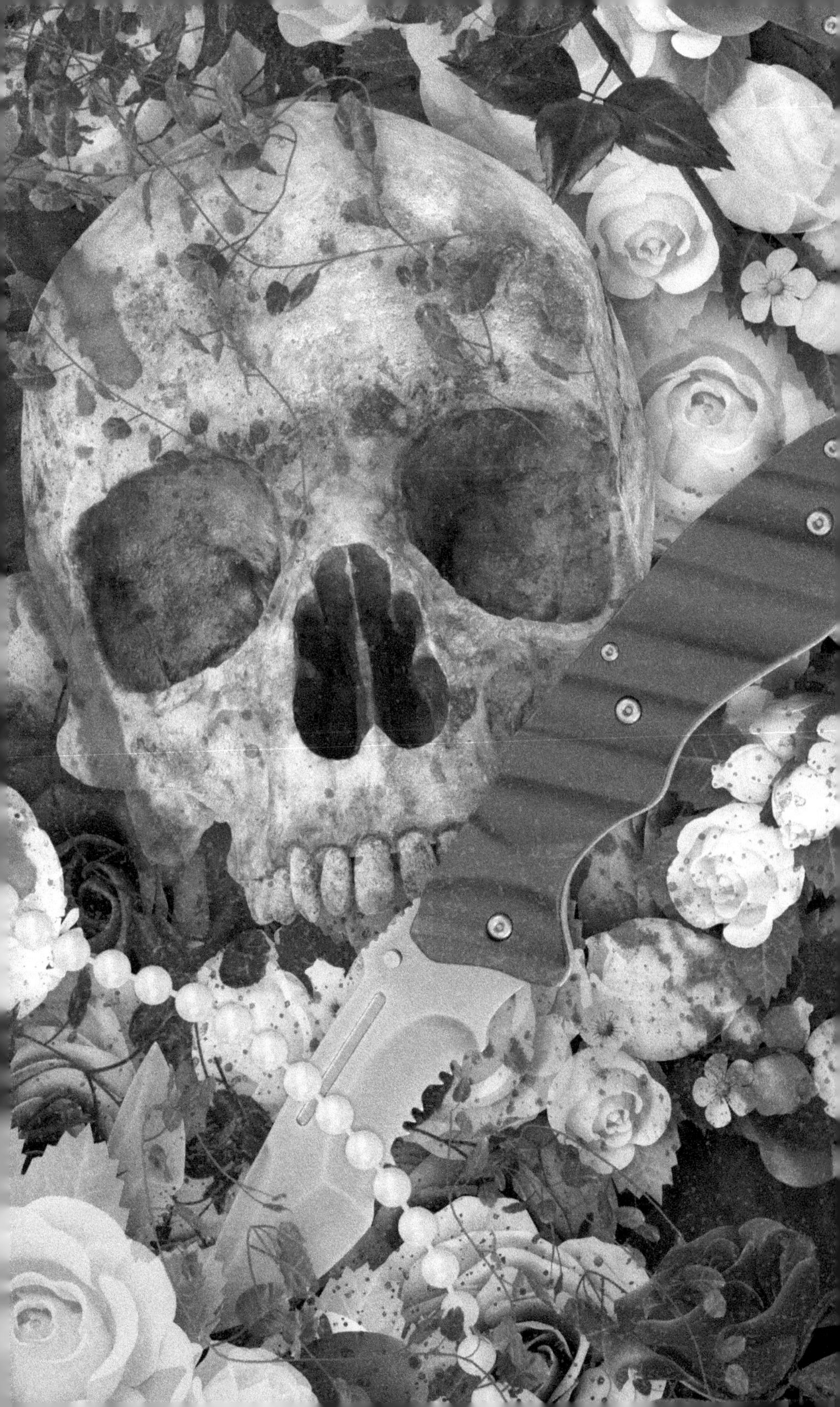

08:45

Six

Jaxon

I'm beyond frustrated. Shortly after I woke up this morning in the guest bedroom, Franklin alerted me to the fact that Melody deleted the app from her phone. It explains why I never received a message last night. What was she thinking?! Was she truly not interested in me, or is it something else? I throw my phone across the room and watch as it hits the wall, and the screen completely shatters.

"Well... now you're going to need a new phone, bro," Franklin states the obvious.

"Not helping, Franklin. Why would she delete the app after swiping right on me? It makes no sense!"

"I don't know man. I don't know how a woman's mind works. They are mysterious creatures."

"I'm not used to this, Franklin. You know how it is at the club every weekend. Women all but throw themselves at me. But not her. She just ran for the hills."

"Yeah, it's strange, I'll give you that. Maybe lay off a bit. Who knows, maybe she'll redownload the app when she has enough time to think it over."

"I want you to consistently monitor her phone and her

whereabouts for me. Set up an alert anytime she is somewhere other than home and relay the info to me. Is that understood?"

"You got it, bro. I'll keep you posted."

Franklin has no idea the lengths I will go to in order to finally grab her attention. Realizing there is nothing more to do right now, I head home, but first stop to get a new phone. I'm tempted to swing by her house, but my resolve can only go for so long. I don't know if I would be able to keep myself from entering her house knowing her tantalizing body is just on the other side of the door.

Pulling up to my building, I turn the car down into the private garage. As I come around the bend, I lower my window and enter in the code. The gate swings open and I'm through. A few more turns and suddenly the motion activated lights are lighting up the room. A few of my most treasured vehicles are within this garage, and the one I'm most interested in right now is my Ducati Panigale V4. It's my favorite vehicle on two wheels. She's sleek, and matte black with red detailing. She has a top speed of 215 mph with restrictions off, not that I've ever gotten her up to that speed. She's my favorite for a reason. I park and exit my BMW and make my way over to the lockers I keep over by the motorcycles. Opening the first locker, I grab out my Dainese Avro leathers and get them on. Not too many wear them out on the road, but when you have a need for speed like I do, you take precautions.

The next thing I grab is my AGV Pista Carbon helmet. She's a sleek black with red details to match the bike. A lot of people ride without a helmet out here in California, but I've never been one to take that risk. My brothers and I have experienced one too many riding buddies that have met a gruesome end without their helmets.

Once I'm all decked out in my riding gear, I start up the Ducati. She purrs to life and it's the most satisfying sound. I swing a leg over and settle into the bike. While gripping the handle bars, I flip the kickstand with my riding boot, gently release the clutch, and I'm gone.

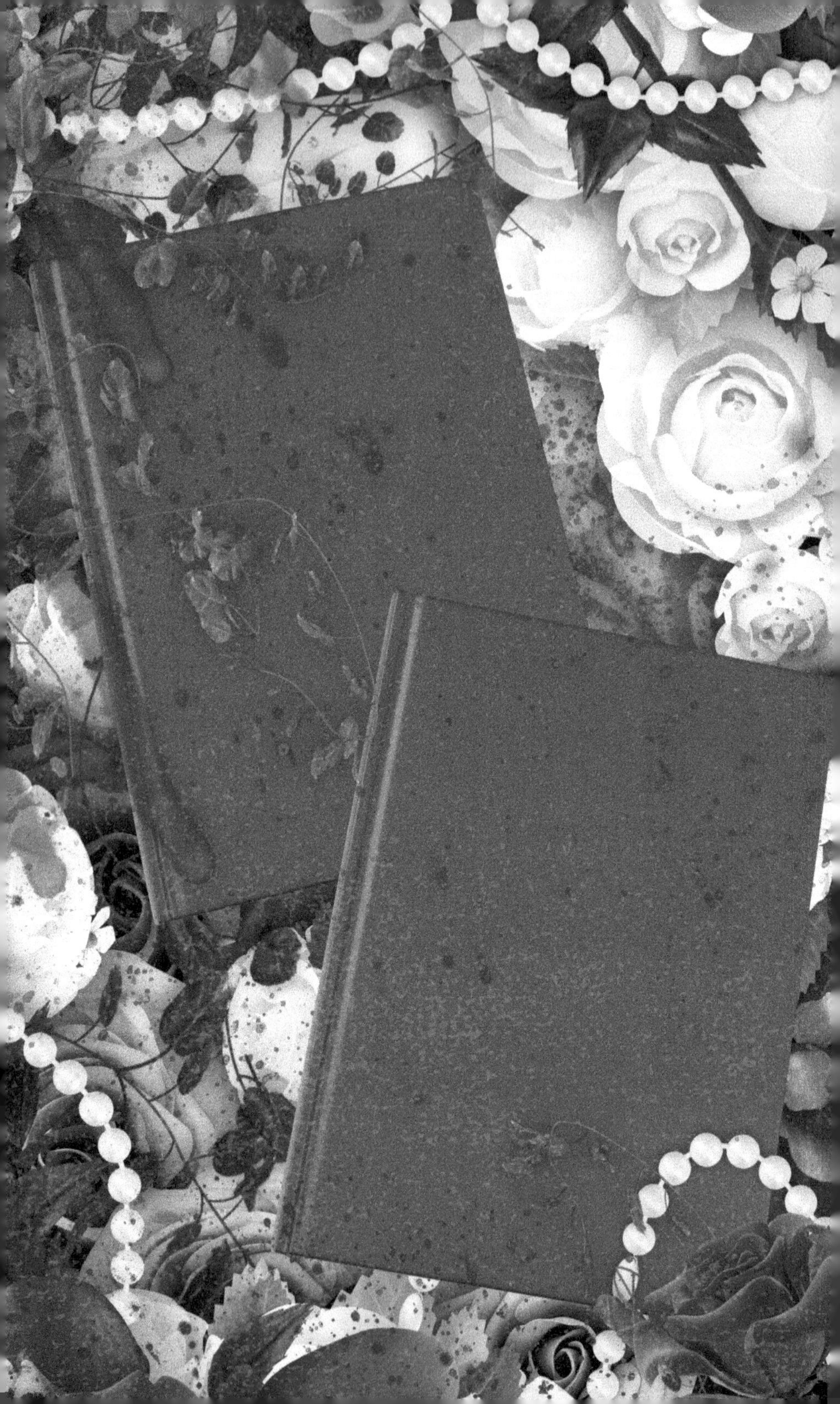

SEVEN
MELODY

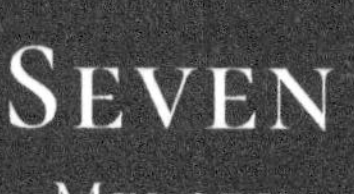

It's a beautiful Sunday evening. I definitely took way too long at the library. Time just completely got away from me. As I stroll back to Main Street, I take in all the twinkling lights strung from each lamp post and the cute little stores. A few people are still milling about and a couple sits close on a bench. I take a deep breath, breathing in the ocean air and the fragrance of freshly cut grass. I love this little town so much. I don't know if I could ever leave it.

While I was in the library, I received a text from my parents asking me to come by for dinner. Wondering what they could possibly be up to, I shot off a text that I would be on my way. Dinner at their house meant I absolutely had to go home and change. Sweatpants and my oversized sweater would not pass their standards.

Pulling into my driveway, I hit the garage opener on my car's visor to open the door. Once I have my car pulled in, I hit the button again. Grabbing my bags and my books, I make my way into my home. She's a simple home, but I love her so much. My parents bought her for me as a graduation present when I finished high school. Over the top? Sure. But they never did anything less than what they thought I deserved.

I have always been riddled with gifts being the only child. When I received my associate's degree, I was gifted my current car, a Mercedes S 580 Sedan. She's black, sleek, and upgraded with all the newest gadgets and gizmos. My parents have always spoiled me, and while it makes me roll my eyes most of the time, I let them do it. Not because I'm a spoiled brat, but because I know my mother's pregnancy with me was very difficult and she almost died. She was told she could never have children again. Hence, why I am their only child.

Dropping my bags off on the couch, I head upstairs and quickly undress. When I'm left in just my panties and my bra, I go into my walk-in closet to see what I can wear. Before I can look any further, however, my eyes catch on one of the tables that holds my jewelry. Sitting on top of the table is a pearl necklace I received from my mom, next to a white rose. My eyes dart back and forth as suddenly, the closet has too many dark corners. I tentatively move forward and inspect the pearls and the rose. I would know the pearls anywhere. But what has me frightened isn't the pearls themselves, it's the fact that someone put them there. I haven't seen these pearls in over a year, since the night that changed my entire life. *What do I do?! Do I call the cops?* They wouldn't believe me even if I tried. The necklace was such a small detail that I never included it in any of my recollections to the investigators.

I slowly back out of my closet, my legs shaking in fear, looking into every corner of my room. What if the person is still in the house? The only person I can think to call is Brooke. Her uncle is a cop, maybe he can dust for prints or something?

The phone rings twice before Brooke's perky voice fills my ear, "Hey girl, what's up?"

"Brooke, I'm sorry but I had no idea who to call. I know your uncle is a cop, I was hoping he could help."

After explaining what happened—minus the events from a year ago—she says they are on their way over. Not trusting my walk-in closet, I head back into my room and throw on my sweat-pants and sweatshirt from earlier today.

Only a few minutes have passed before I hear a knock on my front door. Jumping at the sudden sound, I move to let them in. What I wasn't expecting is the six-foot-something, brown haired, green eyed model that's standing in front of me. He smiles and I immediately pick my mouth up from the floor. Peeking from behind his back is Brooke, and she gives me a little wave.

"Umm, hi, Brooke. Who's this?"

"Sorry, girl, my uncle was busy so you get James instead. He's one of my older brothers."

"Pleasure to meet you, Melody," he says while holding out his hand. He has a slight accent, as though he originated from England, but it's been lessened by living in the states.

"Nice to meet you, James." We shake hands and I move to the side so they can come into my house.

"I'm sorry to have called you, Brooke, but I had no idea who else to call, and I was freaking out..."

She cuts me off before I can continue my nervous blabbering.

"It's all good. James is going to take a look around if you can show him where to go. He's not a cop like Uncle Bill, but he's pretty good at this stuff all the same."

I'm just grateful for anyone to be here right now so I'm not alone. After directing James to my walk-in closet, I send a quick text to my parents letting them know I can't make it tonight and that I'm not feeling well. They text back that they hope I feel better and they hope I can make it next Sunday.

"Well, I can tell you that whoever left these items was very careful. Not a single set of prints that I could get off them, and there appears to be no sign of forced entry anywhere in the house. Though, they could have come in your bedroom window. It was unlocked," James states while coming in the room from upstairs.

"Shit, shit, shit," I start muttering under my breath. How could I be so reckless? I always lock my windows. I don't how I missed it.

"Alright, everything is going to be OK," Brooke says while rubbing circles on my back. "You just take the day off tomorrow. I'll handle the store."

"Are you sure, Brooke? I hate to not come in on my first day on my own."

"Totally fine. You've had quite a scare. Take the day to just relax and maybe look into getting a better security system installed. Though I still think you should call the cops."

"Thank you, Brooke... honestly they would probably think I was losing my mind."

"I agree with Brooke, Miss Harper," says James ever so proper. "At least it will be documented should anything else happen. And I second a much better security system. Yours appears not to be functional at all. I actually know someone that can get it installed for you. Let me give him a quick call."

James leaves the room to call whoever he's going to call, and Brooke comes over to sit at the dining room table with me. I put my head into my hands and just shake my head. "I can't believe this is happening... I should have gotten the security system fixed a long time ago," I say to myself.

Brooke, having seen my collection, grabs a bottle of wine and unscrews the top, handing me over the full bottle. "Girl, you need this right now. No one is judging."

"Thanks, Brooke, for everything. If I tell my parents about this I'll be whisked away faster than you could blink an eye, so telling them is completely out of the question."

"Hey, I totally get it."

"Miss Harper, my contact will be by tomorrow at 9 A.M. to install a new security system for you. The best of the best. His name is Franklin and he has his own security business. He'll get you set up with everything in no time," says James as he walks back into the room.

Feeling tears coming on, I mumble out a quick thank you, give Brooke a hug, and walk them to the front door. "Seriously, thank you both so much."

"No problem, lady. You get some rest now, and just be assured that Franklin will take care of you. He's a long time friend of my brothers, so I know he'll only get you top of the line gadgets," Brooke replies before turning and leaving.

I wave them goodbye and lock the door as well as the deadbolt. I have never felt unsafe in my own house, but I suppose there is a first for everything. As the day starts to catch up with me, I head back up to my bedroom. Now that I can rest assured no one is up here, I head into my walk-in to grab my pajamas. I refuse to even glance at the pearls and rose still on my table.

Once I'm warm and cozy, I cuddle up in bed and stare at my ceiling. I wish I knew who left the pearls, but in reality it can only be one person. What does he want? I ask myself this over and over without a clear answer. The more I think about it though, the angrier I get. How dare he come back after all this time and try to undo all the work I've done on myself. How dare he...

Eventually I fall into a restless sleep.

CHAPTER 7.5
UNKNOWN

PRESENT DAY

Now I have her attention and on our anniversary no less. I knew the pearls would do the trick. I remember back when I took them from her pretty neck, a little parting gift if you will.

Now... well, now she remembers. She's spent the last year trying to forget me, but all of that is going to change.

EIGHT
MELODY

ONE YEAR AGO

It's a warm night in Silicon Valley. My friends Rachel, Alex, and I are all out in the city, bar hopping and dancing the night away.

"Fuck that place, it wasn't good at all. The bouncers were creeps too," says Alex, slurring her words and barely able to stand up straight without swaying on her feet.

Rachel just laughs at her. Alex has always been the dramatic one. I just nod my head and agree with her.

"What do you say we stop at one more bar and then we can head home?" Rachel asks. She doesn't even wait for our reply before she's looping her arms through both of ours, leading the way.

We walk for what feels like forever and my heeled feet are starting to hurt. Though I'm used to wearing heels for special occasions, I am *NOT* used to wearing them out for six plus hours walking to ten different bars.

Finally, we arrive to the bar as announced by Rachel. *Duke's Bar*. Sounds simple enough. The outside is dated, and I can tell this bar is a little more rundown than the rest we were at tonight.

I'm just looking forward to sitting down and getting off my feet though.

Once inside, we beeline straight for the bar and signal the bartender over. Rachel orders a martini neat, Alex orders a whiskey sour, and I just ask for water. The bartender gives me a look but continues on to make the drinks. *Whatever*, I've had enough drinking for one night and I'd prefer to be sober when I catch a ride home. Too many sleazy people in the world that would be more than happy to take advantage of a drunk girl.

A couple of guys make their way over to us, probably to buy us drinks and start some boring conversation before ending it with, "Hey, you wanna get outta here?" It's always the same. I turn away from them and tell the girls I'm going to head out for the night. I use my Uber app to request a ride home. It's not the cheapest but definitely worth not driving drunk.

As we say our goodbyes, I take one last drink of my water, then head outside to wait for the Uber. As I stand waiting, I can hear the music from inside the bar each time the door opens.

"What's a pretty girl like you doing out here all alone?" someone asks from behind me.

As I turn, my world tilts on its axis. I know I wasn't that drunk when I got to the bar and all I had was a water. If anything I should be more sober. It makes me immediately on edge, though it feels like my brain is processing everything extremely slow.

"Imf... note... avone..." I say, slurring my words as the world continues to spin.

"Here, let's sit you down before you fall on that pretty face of yours."

Next thing I know I'm being dragged down the alley next to the bar. I can't make out much of the guy other than he's tall, maybe six foot, wearing a ghost mask with the mesh eye coverings removed, and tattoos all over his arms. I try to fight his grasp, clawing my nails at his arms and hoping beyond hope that someone hears my garbled cries for help. I continue to yell, but no one can hear me; it's useless.

My world erupts into a bright white. Then comes the pain. He hit me with something—a brick maybe? Blood starts running down my face and then I'm slammed up against the wall. He grabs at the hem of my dress, trying to lift it up, grabbing me roughly and scraping my skin. He has one hand on my throat, choking me enough that I'm left gasping for air. He starts to fumble with his belt and I know exactly what he's trying to do. I immediately begin to fight with renewed life, kicking and hitting any part of him that I can. He brings my face up to his masked one, and I can just barely make out the browns of his eyes. They are soulless, and it feels as though he's the reaper coming to claim my soul. Before I can think, he slams my head against the brick building and my world goes black...

08:45

NINE

JAXON

PRESENT DAY

I trailed Melody on the GPS system Franklin installed on my phone for the better part of the day. She went shopping for a bit before getting lost in the library. She was dressed down today, but still looked so effortlessly gorgeous. It took all my restraint not to go in that library and back her into a bookcase, ravishing her body. She was delectable. I can't wait until the day I can mark her as mine.

Later in the evening, she got a text from her parents to have dinner, so I ended my pursuit and headed home. When I got home myself, I reviewed all of her documents again. I was missing something, I just couldn't put my finger on what it was. She was going to school to get her bachelor's degree and she suddenly dropped out. She's been off the grid for the last year. It made no sense, my little sparrow was a straight A student. Why would she suddenly stop? I know that her relationship ended with Brian around that time, but that came a month or two after dropping out. Hmmm, my little sparrow was hiding something and I am going to find out what exactly that is.

Putting her folder down on my desk, I make my way over to

my bar. Grabbing the eighteen-year-old Macallan from the shelf, I pour myself a drink, the ice cubes clinking in the glass. My phone rings, nearly making me drop the glass in my hand.

"This is Jaxon."

"Jax, it's Franklin. You won't believe what I have to tell you."

I sit down behind my desk, setting my drink in front of me. "Spit it out then, Franklin. Why do you sound out of breath?"

"I've just been running around getting the best of my equipment and hacking into it all. I was called up by your brother for a favor. Someone was in Melody's house."

"WHAT?!" I yell into the phone. I'm standing before I can even register the move myself and throwing my glass across the room, the glass exploding off the opposite wall.

"Who was it Franklin? Tell me now, so help me god."

"Well that's the thing, Jax, no one knows who it was, only that Melody was extremely freaked out. I don't know how she knows your brother, but Brooke was there too."

"I need to know everything, Franklin, start from the beginning."

"Well, from what I've gathered, Melody got home and saw a necklace in her closet that she hasn't had in a year. She seemed really spooked that it was back in her possession. I think she knows more than she let on, but James tried to pull fingerprints and didn't get a single one. Whoever left them knew what they were doing."

"Hmmm, what is the significance of those pearls, I wonder?"

"I wondered the same thing, Jax. There was blood on the pearls; I figure it must be something traumatic. So I did a little more digging. I had to expand my search but I did pull up something from Silicon Valley about a year ago. Not sure if it's Melody as they kept her identity hidden, probably paid off, but there was an attack on someone fitting her description outside a sleazy bar in the downtown area. The victim was brutally attacked and raped."

My world spins on its axis and I reach out and brace myself on the desk. My little sparrow... attacked and raped? Melody is as bright as the sun and someone tried to extinguish that. It would explain the dropping out of college and probably why things broke off with her and Brian. Some men are just pieces of shit.

"How did Brooke and James end up there?"

"From what I got from James, apparently Melody is Brooke's newest hire for the bookshop. James tagged along because your Uncle Bill was taking a call."

"Makes sense... How did we not know that my sister hired her?"

"Probably because Brooke is trusting of people to a fault. She never did a background check or any sort of official hiring process."

"I see... So what are you doing with the hardware again?"

"James wanted the best of the best, so he called me. I was thinking you'd probably want to keep tabs on Melody, so I'm installing a link for the cameras to your phone. I just need you to swing by and bring your phone over before 8 A.M. I gotta be there for the install at nine."

"You got it. I'll be there."

We hang up the phone and I'm left pacing in my office. My little sparrow... My chest clenches at the thought of anyone hurting her. I want to protect her at all costs. I don't care if that means I have to intrude on her privacy. No one is going to hurt Melody again, not without answering to me. I will bury them so far in the ground that even the cadaver dogs won't be able to find them.

TEN

MELODY

Knowing that James's connection would be over early as hell to set up the new security system, I set my alarm for 8 A.M. I'm up and getting dressed before 8:30 A.M. and still have thirty minutes before he will be here. If my life wasn't so fucked up, I wouldn't have to go through all this. While I'm downstairs waiting for him, I pour myself a glass of wine and start scrolling on my phone. Who gives a shit that it's eight thirty in the morning.

I start to see ads for Tinder again and figure why the hell not. Fuck it. If I matched with the hottest guy on that app, who cares. Let's give it a go, though it might be the wine talking at this point. I don't care though, this fucker has me scared of my own house, I'll be damned if he prevents me from getting some good dick.

Two glasses of wine later, I'm full on swiping on the app. I've had a few good looking ones message me, but they fell flat after only a few questions. Before I can reply to the next guy, there's a knock on the door. I set down my wine and make my way over, brushing a hand over my attire before swinging open the door.

"Hello, Miss Harper, my name's Franklin. I'm here to install your new security system."

"Hi, Franklin, it's nice to meet you. You can call me Melody.

Please, come in," I reply holding open the door and letting him walk by me.

"So, I'll get to work taking down the old system, setting up the new system for you, and installing all the cameras. Once I'm done, I'll come back and grab you so that I can show you how to work the system and the app if that's ok with you?"

"Perfectly fine, I'll be here in the living room. Thank you so much for coming on such short notice. I really appreciate it."

I sit back in the living room and briefly watch Franklin taking measurements of windows and doorways. *Must be something to do with the system setup.* I shrug my shoulders and move my attention back to Tinder. I've been matched up with Jaxon but he hasn't messaged me yet and I'm definitely not about to be the first one to rock that boat. Though, if I don't find anyone promising on here, at least I have Jaxon's photo to get me through the lonely nights. I blush at the thought alone, or is that the wine?

Before I can give my full attention back to the app, my phone alerts me to a new text message. It's Brooke.

BROOKE

Hey girl, just checking on you and making sure you're okay.

ME

I'm good, thank you for checking in.

Franklin is here installing the new security system as we speak.

BROOKE

Good! He's seriously the best.

You're in good hands.

ME

Thanks Brooke, I should be in tomorrow for work.

BROOKE

Nope, you won't be.

Take another day to settle in.

ME

Brooke, seriously, I'll be fine.

BROOKE

Nope, boss's orders.

See you Wednesday!

CLOSING OUT OF THE CHAT WITH BROOKE, I OPEN UP Tinder and start scrolling. A good two or three hours must pass before I notice Franklin standing in the entryway with all his tools in his hands.

"Is everything finished," I ask, getting up from the couch. I'm a little tipsy, but nothing noticeable.

"Yes, ma'am. I was going to show you the system if now is an OK time?"

"Sure."

Franklin proceeds to show me the system, how to turn on and off the alarm, how to set zones, and how to view the camera feed. There is a camera in the front and back yard as well as in every single room of the house, including my bedroom. I start to protest that camera, but Franklin reassures me it is necessary seeing that whoever came in probably used my bedroom window. He assures me that whoever came in here would not be able to get into the camera system.

I am instantly relieved at that; I don't want some creepy fuck watching me as I sleep, or worse... The system is set to continuously record for one week before the system stops and restarts a fresh recording. It means it would allow me access to footage taken up to a week prior if I want to review it or save anything. Thoroughly impressed, I thank Franklin and ask what method of payment he prefers.

"Oh, no, ma'am. That has been taken care of by the Stonewells, no need to worry about payment."

"What?! They did NOT!"

"Truly they did. They mean well. Best bet is just to accept it graciously. That family is loaded."

While I accept that fact and thank Franklin for his time and work, I know I will be having a word with Brooke come Wednesday.

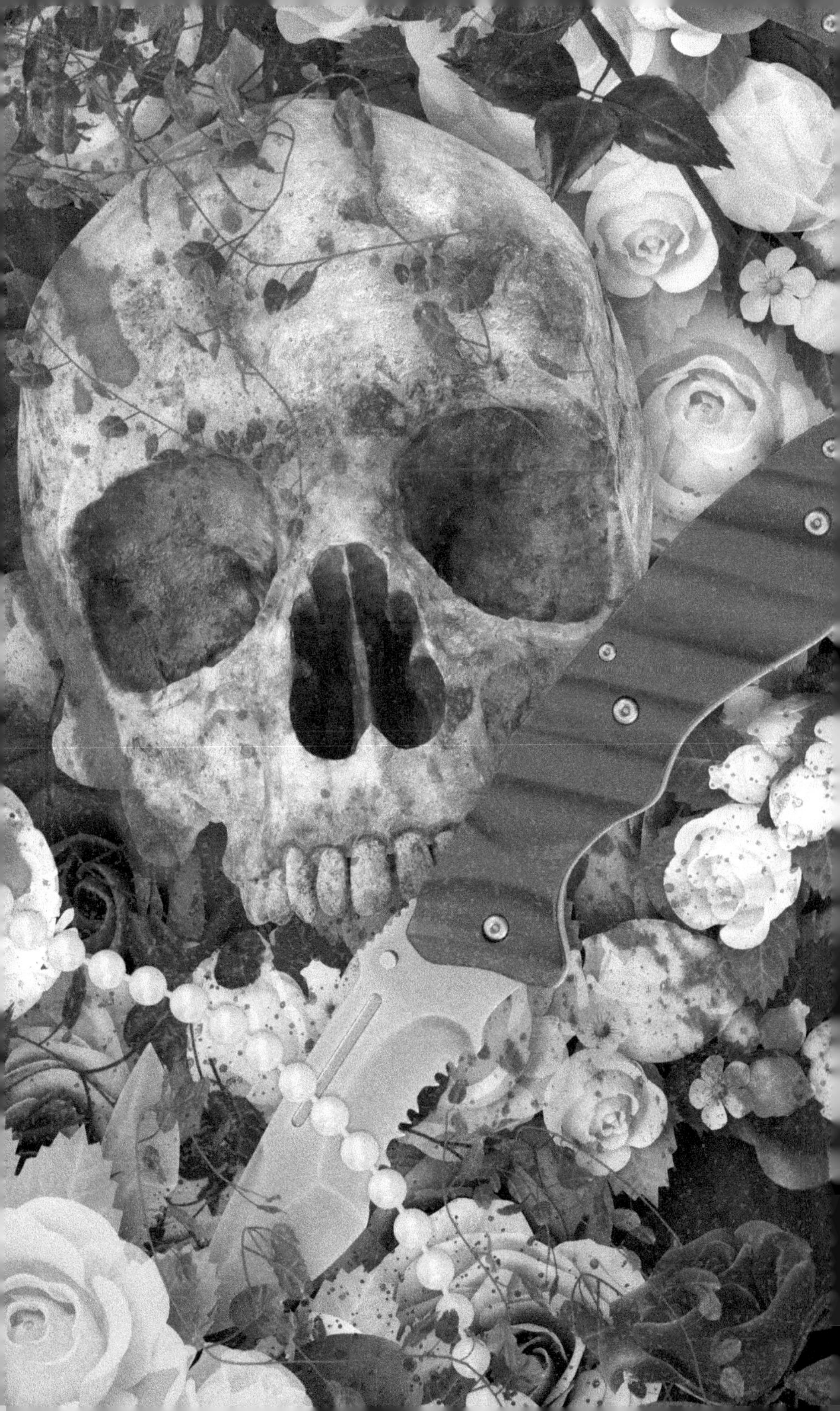

ELEVEN

JAXON

Franklin calls me on his way home from Melody's place.

"Dude, you gotta check the cams. When I got there, she was pretty tipsy, though I think she thought she hid it well enough. She might be going off the deep end over there. Oh, and while I was on my way home, I got an alert that she reinstalled Tinder." Franklin laughs, but I don't find it funny at all. My little sparrow is hurting and this is how she's processing it.

"Right. Let me get off the phone with you, I'll check the feeds," I reply back, hanging up the phone before he can get another word in. Franklin means well but sometimes he can be so clueless to certain things. Women being one of them.

I know my little sparrow. She's not handling this very well. I take it wine is her best friend when her emotions are too big for her.

Tapping into the app on my phone, I click on the camera that shows a still of Melody sitting on her couch. Franklin put a damn camera in every room in the house. I can't be mad at him though. Now I'll always know where she is and what she's doing in that house of hers.

I watch as Melody seems to be scrolling on her phone, though I can't see from this angle what she is scrolling on. With a huff, she gets up, tells her Alexa to play some '90s hip hop, and off she goes dancing from room to room. My little sparrow has no inhibitions right now, she's completely free, moving to the music as she goes. She's a wonder to behold. Even though I know she is processing everything a little different than anyone else, I adore seeing this side of her. The side where she completely lets loose.

This continues for a good forty minutes, and I'm transfixed by her for every single one of those minutes. She grabs what's left of her wine bottle in the kitchen and moves towards the living room. Switching the camera feed to the living room, I watch as she drinks straight from the bottle before laying down with a comfy blanket and bringing up her phone again.

Figuring now is the perfect time to catch her reaction, I quickly split screen the apps and pull up Tinder. I shoot her a message, watching the camera for how this affects her. The response is immediate. She tenses, releasing her phone into her lap, and dropping her head back on the couch pillow. My little sparrow is flustered. I shoot off a second message and finally get a reply.

ME

Hello beautiful.

Not gonna say hi to me?

MELODY

Hi there Jaxon. How are you?

ME

I'm pretty good. I see that we matched on this app, huh?

MELODY

Nice way to state the obvious.

I think the app made a mistake though.

ME

Why would you think that?

MELODY

Because I don't seem like your type.

ME

What do you think my type is?

MELODY

IDK, blonde hair, blue eyes, perky tits and hour glass figure.

ME

Well, Melody, I swiped right on you for a reason.

MELODY

And what might that reason be?

ME

Well for starters your beautiful green eyes.

You seem to have a love for reading, which I also love to do. And your curves might not be hourglass, but they sure do something to me.

MELODY

You're just saying that.

You could probably have any woman on this app.

ME

Well, Melody, you're the only one I want and when I want something, I take it.

MELODY

What if I'm not available to be taken?

ME

Oh you are, otherwise you wouldn't be on this app.

MELODY

True...

I sit back and watch her reactions on the camera. The more we chat, the straighter she sits up. To say I have her attention would be an understatement. She's playing hard to get, but what my little sparrow doesn't know is that she's already mine. It's just going to take some time and finesse to get her to realize it.

I leave her on read to see what she will do. A few times I see the dots in the corner that means she's typing, but they keep disappearing, as though she keeps changing her mind on what to say. She sets down her phone and finishes off her wine, drinking straight from the bottle. What I wouldn't give to know what my little sparrow is thinking right now. Does she want me as bad as I want her?

ME

See, Melody, I'm glad we matched up.

MELODY

Oh really? *Smirk face*

ME

Yep. Soon, you'll be all mine. *devil horn face*

MELODY

Prove it. *wink face*

My little sparrow is playing with fire. It must be the alcohol giving her some liquid courage. From what I've seen so far, Melody is shy and reserved. I'm enjoying this side of her, this side she keeps hidden from the light.

ME

How do you want me to prove it?

MELODY

IDK, use your imagination.

ME

Melody, Melody, Melody.

You sure are a little brat, aren't you? Speaking to me like that, I should put you over my knee. Spank the sass right out of you.

MELODY

Hmmmm, IDK if you could handle all of this.

ME

Melody, I will handle you right on this dick, leaving you panting and wanting more. Should I continue?

At this point, my cock is straining against my jean zipper. I'm agonizingly hard. I palm myself through my jeans, anything to relieve some of the tension that is building up.

Yes, please.

Melody gets up and brings the wine bottle to the kitchen. She makes her way toward the stairs and I have to switch the camera feed. I check the hall camera and just see her slip into her bedroom. *What are you doing, little sparrow?*

Once I have her bedroom camera pulled up, I see her sashay her way into her closet. She comes out in nothing but a lacy bra and panties. Matching. If my dick could get any harder, I'd be busting out of these jeans. Melody is damn breathtaking. She climbs into bed, leaving the blankets off so I have a full view of her splayed out like a meal. She holds me so transfixed I almost miss the message she sends, knocking me back to my senses.

MELODY

Are you still there?

ME

Oh, I'm still here, little sparrow.

Do you want to know what I'd do with that sassy mouth of yours?

MELODY

Maybe. Though be careful, I have teeth.

ME

Nothing like a little bit of pain, am I right?

MELODY

Pain and pleasure go hand in hand, most would say.

ME

Mmmm, I plan on wringing every bit of pleasure from that delectable body of yours.

Send me a pic, remind me whose body I'm pleasuring. *wink face*

Melody stares at the phone for a minute before raising her phone above her head and snaps a few photos. After what feels like forever, she must finally settle on the one she likes best, because next thing I know my phone is alerting me to her new message.

I click open the image and groan at the sight before me. It's one thing to view her on the camera, but to have an overview shot of her, like I'm the one over her body staring down at her, makes it feel that much more real. Her breasts are spilling over her lacy bra and she's staring at the camera like she's ready to be fucked within an inch of her life. She's biting her lip, too. Oh, my little sparrow knows exactly what she's doing to me.

Before I can type a reply, I notice Melody reach into her nightstand and pull out something round and pink. She starts to slowly rub her breasts, grabbing and teasing through her bra. Her head falls back against the pillow and she runs her hands down her stomach.

Melody is fucking getting off to me right now. Knowing I hold all the cards, I type out a reply to get her attention.

ME

You don't come unless I tell you.

Is that understood little sparrow?

MELODY

Yes sir.

ME

What are you wearing with that pink bra?

MELODY

Wouldn't you like to know...

wink face a pink thong.

ME

Mmmm... Spread your legs.

I want you to slowly run your hand up your inner thigh, then do the same to the other thigh. Do NOT touch that pretty pussy yet.

MELODY

OK.

She runs her hands along her inner thighs like I told her to. I can't stand to see Melody pleasuring herself and not do the same. Unzipping my jeans, I pull them and my briefs halfway down my thighs, just enough to get them past my raging erection and finally release my cock. I give it one, two strokes before I stop.

ME

Does that feel good baby? Do you like the feel of my hands on those delicious thighs?

Do you want more?

MELODY

God, yes please.

ME

I may not be god, but when I'm done with you, it will be me you're praying to.

I continue stroking my cock lazily as I watch her continue to stroke her thighs. She pauses, as though she's waiting for my next command.

ME

Take your hand and run it up your stomach, squeezing your waist as you go. I want you to slip your hand under your bra, teasing your nipple in slow circles before giving it a pinch.

Melody listens to directions so well. She may be a brat, but with my instructions she's perfectly submissive to my every demand.

Her body arches when she pinches her nipple, a little moan slipping out from between her lips. She's rubbing her thighs together, chasing whatever friction she can get.

At her moan, I almost lose it. My grip on my cock tightens and I'm fighting the urge to pump myself hard and fast. But not yet.

That feels so good.

Mmm, I growl. So Melody likes to be instructed in the bedroom... that I can most certainly work with.

ME

What a good girl.

MELODY

Ohhh *surprised face*

ME

Oh you like that huh? My little bird has a praise kink?

MELODY

Maybe…

ME

Well why don't you be a good girl and play with that pretty pussy?

MELODY

smirk face

I watch on the camera feed as Melody slips her panties down her legs, throws them aside, and brings the toy to her perfect pussy. I can hear the vibrations through the camera feed. She must have it cranked up to one of the higher settings.

As she takes her toy and makes slow circles around her clit, I see her use her other hand to wrap around her throat. So my little sparrow enjoys a hand necklace? Good to know. Melody pauses her ministrations and types out a message.

MELODY

I want to come.

ME

Not yet you aren't.

Stop what you're doing.

MELODY

OK. Tell me what you want,

I was so close. *sobbing face*

I want you to get on all fours and set your phone on the pillows so you can see my instructions. Take your left hand and grab the headboard, and with your right hand, play with that pretty pussy. Imagine you're sitting on my face. My tongue is licking you, sucking your clit.

I watch her on the camera, grinding her toy on her pussy, while her hips are flexing with pleasure. I start to stroke myself again, using the bead of pre-cum at the tip to lubricate my entire dick. What I wouldn't give to have her pretty little cunt wrapped around my dick instead of my hand.

Come baby, come until you're dripping down my face.

Her motions become choppy as she nears her orgasm. She throws her head back and with one final jerk of her hips, she's falling. The little moans of pleasure falling from her beautiful lips are all I need to spur myself on. A few more strokes and I'm falling with her, hot spurts of cum covering my hand and jeans. Her name falls from my lips so easily.

Melody takes a minute or two to compose herself before grabbing her phone again.

Hot drool face Thank you. That was… hot.

I'm glad I could be of service, though

I got my enjoyment out of it as much as you did.

Is that right?

Did I make you hard, Jaxon?

ME

Oh, baby girl, you did more than make me hard.

The mess I have to clean up attests to that.

Maybe next time it could be in person?

MELODY

shocked face Ohhhh.

I'll think about it, k?

ME

I can be patient, little sparrow. *smirk face*

MELODY

wink face

As I watch the camera feed, Melody gets out of bed and cleans herself up in her bathroom and washes her toy before climbing back into bed, this time in pajamas.

She has absolutely no idea just how patient I can be for her.

Twelve

MELODY

I wake up to sunlight streaming right in my face. With a groan, I roll over towards my window and yank the curtain closed. Holy shit balls, that was bright as hell, and my head is pounding. Maybe indulging in wine at 9 A.M. wasn't my smartest decision.

Grabbing my phone, I check the time and see it's 3:15 P.M. I don't even recall going to sleep. I remember Franklin coming over and leaving, dancing, drinking wine, and then sitting on the couch and getting a message from Jaxon. Everything after that is completely blank. Opening up Tinder, I see Jaxon's face at the top of my message folder. God, he's so handsome. I could get lost in his silvery blue eyes any day.

Upon opening the message thread, I'm immediately horrified by the length of the conversation. *Jeeze, what did I say to this man*? I scroll as fast as I can all the way to the beginning and start there. The more I read, the more embarrassed I'm getting. I cannot believe I sexted a complete stranger. A hot stranger, but a stranger nonetheless. O-M-G... *I have a praise kink*?! I'm morti-fied. Absolutely mortified.

I'll never meet him in person right? Yeah, probably not. I'll be fine. *FUCK*. What if I do though? No, I can't manifest it. I won't ever meet him. *Oh my god*. A thought just crossed my mind. What if I've been catfished and that isn't Jaxon at all, but some random guy that enjoys getting girls off? God, I really hope I haven't been catfished. That would somehow be even more embarrassing.

Getting up and tossing my phone on the bed, I head to the bathroom to get washed up and take some ibuprofen for this killer headache. When I get back in the bedroom, I see a new Tinder alert on my phone. Instantly nervous, a blush breaking out over my face and chest, I grab my phone and open the app. I'm not at all surprised that it's from Jaxon.

JAXON

Hey beautiful

ME

Hi Jaxon.

JAXON

How are you?

Ignoring his question, I get right to the point.

ME

How do I know you aren't a fake? You could be catfishing me.

JAXON

What can I do to prove it to you, little sparrow?

ME

Write my name on a piece of paper with today's date and hold it up to your face.

I wait a few minutes, setting my phone down because at this point this man has me hanging on his every word, and I don't want to get too attached too quickly.

JAXON

Here you go babe.

picture

Though I'd much rather prove it by taking you
out on a date.

ME

OK, so you're definitely the real deal. Good to
know.

JAXON

Are we not going to talk about what happened
earlier today?

ME

I'd actually prefer that we didn't. I was drunk
and clearly didn't know any better.

JAXON

Oh Melody, but I gave you one of the best
orgasms of your life without even touching
you.

That's definitely something we should talk
about.

ME

Ugh, OK yes, I won't disagree with you. But I
don't remember any of it, so according to
those rules, I actually haven't experienced an
orgasm by you yet.

Was I poking the bear? Maybe yes, but let's see what he has to say for himself. I am somewhat relieved that he's real, but where do we go from here? There is obviously physical attraction. Do we go out on dates? I don't know how to navigate dating life, it's been too long since I've done this whole *getting to know someone* thing.

Plus there's the fact that I have a stalker, AKA my attacker. I don't want anyone else getting hurt because of me. What if he goes after the people I care about... I probably shouldn't pursue anything with Jaxon just yet.

JAXON

Is that so, little sparrow?

Well, we need to rectify that, and soon.

Can I take you out? Get to know you?

ME

Ya know, I'm not sure it's the best idea right now. I have a lot going on in my personal life and I'm not sure I'm ready for anything that requires commitment.

JAXON

Fair enough, Melody.

Fair enough. I'll be waiting, though. I'm a patient man, but eventually I always get what I want.

He sure is cocky, but his words send a thrill through my body. I'm finding that I don't want our conversation to end. I'd love nothing more than to get to know him, but it's probably for the best right now.

THE REST OF THE WEEK PASSES IN A BLUR. JAXON AND I talk everyday, it's kind of become the new norm. We talk about my time in school and all the late nights studying in the school library with Rachel, Alex, and Damian. I tell Jaxon that I took time off from school but don't go too far into detail. We talk about his work in the finance and investment world and where he grew up. I wake up to his texts and I even go to bed with *good night* texts. It's cute really. I'm not sure where things are headed, but I'm enjoying the moment and taking it one day at a time.

I got back to work on Wednesday and Brooke showed me the ropes again. Thursday and Friday I got to work in the shop by myself, which went amazingly well. Today, I'm doing much of the same. People that love books just seem so nice. I know working in retail can be hard, but selling books is so pleasant.

Just as I'm about to close up the shop for the day, Brooke walks in, a big smile on her face. She has a mischievous twinkle in her eye, and I don't know if I want to know what she has up her sleeve.

"So, Melody... I was hoping I could convince you to come out to Club LAX with me tonight."

Before I can even respond, she's rattling off, speaking so fast I can barely keep up.

"My brother owns the club, and they always have the best DJ on Saturday nights. I can get us a VIP booth and everything! Even free drinks!"

"I don't know, Brooke," I reply tentatively. I haven't been out to bars or clubs since that night, and the idea makes me nervous, my stomach doing flips.

"Oh come on, Melody. It's good to get out every once in a while. Reading is good and fun, but sometimes you need to just let loose a little, girl!" She grabs my arm on that last bit, shaking me excitedly.

"Alright alright, I'll go out with you, but I don't want to be out too late."

"Perfect, I brought all my stuff with me, let's get ready at your place," she says over her shoulder, already headed for the door.

"OK, let me lock up real quick."

After I lock up the store, we both take our separate vehicles and head to my home. Traffic is light so we make it to my place in record time. After parking in the garage, we both make our way inside. I disarm the security system when we get in, and place my bag and coat on the table.

"I see the security system Franklin installed is working nicely."

"It is, thank you by the way. I wish you all wouldn't have paid for it. I feel like I owe you guys now."

"Not at all lady. My brother is loaded, and I mean loaded. It was probably a penny in the bucket for him honestly."

"If you say so. So what is this club we're going to again?" I ask as I lead us upstairs into my bedroom. Good thing I decided to make my bed today. I do a quick check and don't see any bras or underwear laying on the floor. *Phew*. All is good.

"It's Club LAX, owned by my brother, Kayden. The only time we ever really see him is when we go to the club. He's not one for family get-togethers."

"Huh... So I'll finally get to meet another brother? Will this one be just as handsome as the last?"

"Honestly, the three of them get a lot of girls. The girls at the club all but throw themselves at them. It's embarrassing really."

"Wow, I can only imagine," I reply, letting out a slight scoff. Seems like not only is the family graced with money, but also with good looks.

As we both start getting ready, I let Brooke raid my closet for what she thinks I should wear. I have plenty of options for plus size women like myself, but some of them are a little too revealing for what I'm comfortable with these days. I'm hoping she chooses one that is more modest.

"Alright, you *HAVE* to wear this one. It's so gorgeous and your ass will look amazing in it." She pulls out one of my ruched dresses that comes to about mid thigh and is black as midnight. It's definitely not a dress to go bending over in, but it's more modest than most in the closet. Plus, because it's ruched, I don't have to wear any of my shape wear with it. It has a low revealing neckline and long sleeves. The long sleeves are a plus because I really don't want to have to explain or receive pity for the scars on my wrists.

Once we are all dressed up, makeup done, and hair styled, we head downstairs.

"You know, maybe we should just get an Uber. That way we both can drink and not worry about how to get back home," Brooke suggests.

"Sounds good to me. You're going to crash here for the night, right?"

"Absolutely, girls night all the way through to tomorrow. Should we do a shot before we leave? Get a little loosened up?" Brooke always has the brightest ideas.

I grab two shot glasses from my cupboard and a bottle of cherry vodka. I pour us both a generous amount and we clink glasses. Bottoms up! My phone lights up with a Tinder alert, and I open it up. It's Jaxon.

JAXON

Any plans on this gorgeous Saturday night?

I could pick you up.

I smile to myself and let a little laugh slip.

ME

Sorry Jaxon, I'm going out for a girl's night with my boss.

Rain check?

I try to let him down easy without completely shutting him down. I enjoy talking to him, but I'm not sure I'm ready for anything serious just yet.

JAXON

Sounds good, little sparrow.

I'll be seeing you.

I still don't know why he calls me little sparrow. I shrug my shoulders. Save that conversation for next time.

"What is making you smile like that?!" Brooke exclaims and just about topples me over trying to get a look at my phone.

I quickly close out of the app. "Nothing, just a guy I've been talking to is all."

"What? Get out! Is he going to meet up with us or what?"

"No no. I told him it's a girl's night. I gave him a rain check for another time."

Feeling the burning sensation in my stomach, my resolve is officially loosened. I am ready to dance the night away, and I'll be damned if my attacker prevents me from living my life.

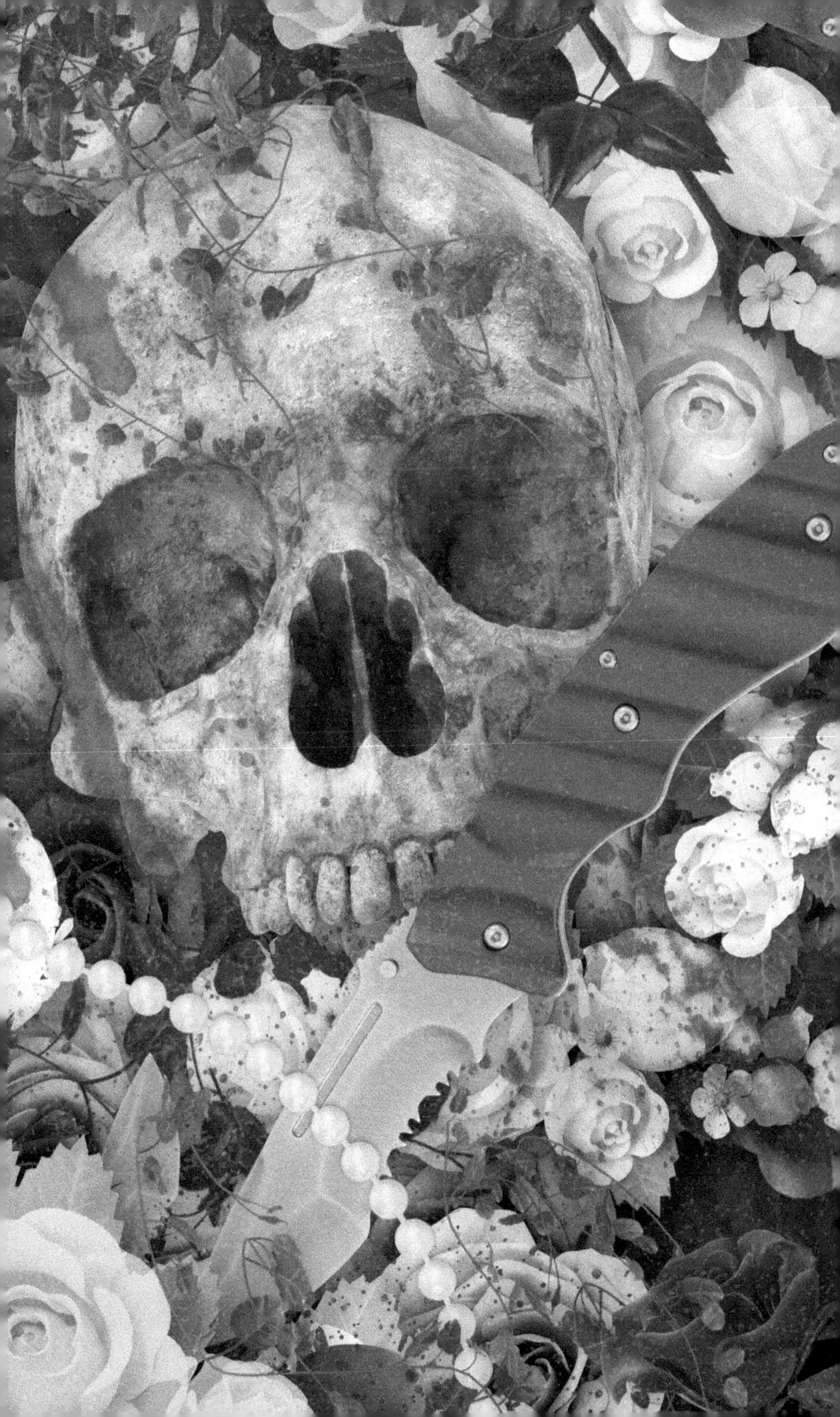

08:45

THIRTEEN

JAXON

Watching Brooke and Melody get ready is very entertaining. I watch them through the camera feed as they sing and dance while getting ready, and then take some shots. I caught the bit about them heading to my brother's club in the city. *Looks like I have plans after all.*

I put on my black slacks and a tucked black, button down shirt with the sleeves rolled and the first two buttons undone. This look allows me to have some of my tattoos on display. I head down to the garage to drive one of my more showy vehicles for the night. My McLaren 675LT is a sleek Volcano Yellow, and one I reserve for nights out on the town or at the club.

Revving the engine, I take off for the club knowing I'll be there much sooner than the ladies. Traffic is heavy for a Saturday night, but nothing this beauty of a car can't handle. I weave in and out of traffic and get to Club LAX with time to spare.

Pulling up to the club, I exit my vehicle and give the keys to the valet. Normally I wouldn't trust a valet, but this is my brother's club, and the staff are well aware of who family is. Walking up to the door, the bouncer immediately waves me through. As I make my way through the crowd, I spot Kayden up on the balcony in the VIP section with a woman on his arm, whispering in his ear. Probably trying to get him to give her a quickie in his office. Knowing Kayden, he'll probably give her exactly what she wants. He is definitely the playboy out of the three of us.

Making my way up the stairs, Mikey, the bartender, waves to me with a questioning look. Normally I'd beeline straight to the bar for a drink, but tonight, I need to be sober. I need to have all my senses while I track my little sparrow throughout the club tonight. Pulling up my phone, I see from the tracker on her phone that she is about ten minutes out from arriving.

Sitting back in the VIP booth that has a clear view of the entrance, I lay my arms on the back of the couch and lean back, waiting for her to make an appearance.

SHE'S BREATHTAKING. WEARING A SHORT BLACK DRESS that leaves just enough to the imagination and high heels that make me imagine those legs wrapped around my hips, grinding that hot pussy on my cock. *I really need to get it together.* She hasn't been in my sights for more than two minutes and I'm already imagining all the dirty things I want to do to her. Watching as the girls order drinks by the bar, I adjust myself in my pants. Melody fucking does something to me.

After the girls get their drinks, they make their way to the VIP section directly across the club from me. They sit in a booth and start chatting animatedly and sipping on their drinks. I continue watching and even the way she sucks on her straw has me losing my mind. What I wouldn't give to have those lips wrapped around my cock.

After two more drinks and two shots each, they make their way down to the dance floor. I make my way to the balcony to keep an eye on them. Melody moves her hips like a goddess. She and Brooke immediately gain the attention of the men around them, including the men here with a date. They are having the time of their lives. To see Melody so careless and free is intoxicating. Her very essence just radiates around her. Gravitating towards her, I place my arms on the railing to watch Melody as she dances and sways around those nearest her.

As they continue dancing, I see two men move in on Brooke and my little sparrow. It starts innocently enough, but soon the distance between Melody and this douche is little to none. I'm clenching my fists with barely controlled fury. How dare he touch what is mine. I see Melody swat his hand away when he confidently puts it on her hip, way too close to her ass. What I didn't see coming is the man almost stops in his tracks before he grabs her hips more forcefully and grinds into her ass.

That's it. There's only so much I can take. I make my way down to the dance floor, weaving in and out of the throngs of dancing bodies. Once I'm close enough I put a hand on the guy's shoulder and spin him around. Before he can say anything, recognition flickers in his eyes and his words die on his tongue. He holds his hands up, and being a very smart man, walks away. I memorize his features; I'll deal with him later.

Given the opportunity, I move in behind Melody putting a hand lightly on her hip, dancing with her before leaning down and whispering in her ear, "Hello, little sparrow."

Fourteen

Melody

Dancing with Brooke is the most free I've felt in a long time. We had drinks in the VIP booth she was able to secure, and we talked about anything and everything. I felt so comfortable with Brooke that I ended up spilling to her that I was attacked a year ago, but I didn't go into any more detail. She could probably guess the gist of it. Brooke lent her sympathy and quickly ordered us two shots. We toasted to *"FUCK THAT ASSHOLE"* before downing one after the other.

Feeling the alcohol kick in and the lights start to blur around us, we make our way down to the dance floor. Brooke was right, their DJ is incredible. We dance around each other, gaining the attention of the surrounding men who are more than eager to join us. Brooke looks over at me and laughs, enjoying every second of the attention. She quickly spins around, giving me her back so that she can dance with the man in front of her, basically grinding on his cock. *Whatever girl, get it.*

The man I am dancing with is very handsy. I've managed to avoid his grasp for the most part, but when the song changes he places his hands on my hips. Not liking the contact, I brush his hand off but continue dancing, hoping he gets the hint. Before I know it, he grabs my hip, biting into my tender flesh and starts grinding his semi-erect dick on my ass. Before I can shove him off, his presence is gone and the energy shifts. I can feel without even looking that someone else is dancing with me now. Not really caring as long as they don't grab me like that fucker did, I continue dancing.

They place a hand lightly on my hip, not at all forcefully like the other guy, and I find that I'm welcoming it. We dance for a few beats and I feel him lean over my right shoulder. My skin breaks out in goosebumps, and I'm instantly turned on. *What is wrong with me?!* Before I can turn around, he leans in to me and whispers, "Hello, little sparrow."

MY BRAIN FREEZES THEN WARPS INTO HYPER SPEED, catching up with the man's words. I turn so fast I'm surprised I don't have whiplash. My eyes collide with the most captivating light blue eyes I've ever seen. My face must look hysterical because I can't believe this is happening. How did he know I was here?! I never mentioned to him where we were going. He continues dancing with me, grabbing my arms and placing them around his neck. He's wearing a cocky smirk on his face like he's won a prize.

I can't even stutter out a reply, I'm in such disbelief. When he continues dancing, his hands on my hips, I give in and start dancing with him. The energy between us is electrifying. Every part of my body he touches leaves a trail of fire in its wake. He lightly brushes his fingers down my arms, and I shiver with the feeling that it elicits. He leans down again, trapping me in his silvery-blue eyes. I turn my head to give him my ear, listening intently to what he has to say.

"Little sparrow, I've finally caught you. Now what am I to do with you?"

My mouth opens to reply but nothing comes out. His hand

moves to my lower back, and he drags me closer, so close I can feel his erection rubbing on my lower stomach. My eyes widen at the contact, but in reality I am so turned on right now.

"Maybe somewhere a little more private," I reply, shouting over the thrumming base of the music. Before he replies, I turn around and tap Brooke on the shoulder to get her attention. When she turns around, I let her know I'm going back up to the VIP booth. She looks behind me and her eyes widen before narrowing. She reaches over me and hits Jaxon.

"What the hell are you doing here, Jaxon? Can't I have one night out on my own?!" she yells over the music.

Confused by how they know each other, I look from Brooke to Jaxon.

Taking pity on my confusion, Jaxon leans down to me and shouts, "That's my sister!"

Everything clicks into place and I can't believe how small the world really is. What are the chances? Something must click into place for Brooke too, because she leans over and shouts into my ear, "Is this the guy you were talking to earlier at the house?"

I nod my head and have the gall to look at her sheepishly.

"I didn't know he was your brother," I shout back.

"We are going to go up to the VIP booth to cool down a bit," I shout again at her.

Brooke looks like she is going to protest before she levels a look at Jaxon. If looks could kill, he'd be dead three times over right now.

Jaxon merely smirks and lets out a chuckle that I can't hear, but I clearly see. He takes my hand and leads me through the crowd. As we reach the stairs, he gestures for me to go first, placing a hand on my back as I pass in front of him. Feeling completely out of my element, I climb the stairs. When we reach the second floor balcony, I turn to look at him, hoping he takes the lead to what booth we should be going to. Jaxon cuts in front of me, taking my hand again, and leads me along to a darker part of the VIP section. While the music is still loud up here, we can at least hear conversations and only have to talk a little louder than normal.

When Jaxon finds what he's looking for, he leads me to a booth in the corner of the second floor, set back into the shadows almost completely unnoticeable. As we get close to the booth, Jaxon gestures for me to sit first. I scoot my way into the circular booth, settling into the middle portion of the seat. Jaxon joins me, scooting his way in to sit next to me.

"Liking the club so far?" he asks while leaning back in the seat, bringing one arm around to the back of the booth. With his other hand, he starts to make slow circles on my leg. While the contact isn't unwanted, it feels dangerous. Like I could combust and set this whole damn club on fire. His touch is intoxicating, and I think he knows it by the smirk on his face.

I blush and look down at my hands in my lap, too nervous to speak. Jaxon takes his hand and lifts my chin, leveling me with a searing look.

"Melody, are you OK?" he asks, concern overtaking his features.

"No, no, I'm fine. Just still in shock that we are meeting like this."

"It was meant to be, little sparrow."

"Why do you call me that?!"

"What? Little sparrow?" he asks.

"Yes, that. Why?"

"You just remind me of an innocent little bird."

"So you say. How did you know where I would be?"

"I didn't. This is my brother's club. I come here every weekend."

Feeling stupid that it's such an obvious answer, I focus on the crowd in front of us. Jaxon isn't having that though, he grabs my chin and turns me to look at him.

"Does that bother you, little sparrow?"

Does it bother me? I have a flash of jealousy when I think

about how many women he must pick up from here, but I quickly squash it down.

"Not really, it's just a weird coincidence. I tend not to believe in them."

"Rest assured, I did not stalk you here," he states, calming my nerves.

I take a good look at Jaxon then. He's undeniably attractive, and I gravitate toward him so easily. The physical attraction that was present over the internet is tenfold in person. We talk a little more, discussing our likes and dislikes. All the while, he continues using his free hand to make small circles on my thigh.

Conversation with Jaxon is easy, a lot easier than I thought it was going to be. I thought I would feel embarrassed because of the sexting, but I'm not, surprisingly.

"So, Melody, what brought you here to Club LAX?"

"Just needed a night out is all. It's been a stressful week to say the least."

He leans over and whispers in my ear, "Can I help take some of that stress away..."

I bite my lip, contemplating his words. Jaxon all but groans before taking a hand and tangling it in my long hair. Tugging me closer to him, he whispers, "Don't bite your lip unless you want me to take you right here in this booth."

My eyes widen at his words, my cheeks flushing scarlet from the promise they hold. I bite my lip again without even thinking, and before I realize what is happening, Jaxon's lips crash into mine. The kiss is scorching, his tongue sweeping my lips, begging for entrance. I meet his tongue with my own, and I swear fireworks are going off behind my eyelids. His tongue dances with mine and I'm moaning. Jaxon captures my moan with his mouth, biting my lip gently and pulling slightly. I hiss through my teeth. That was such a turn on. I'm pretty sure my panties are soaked by now, and I blush from the thought alone.

Jaxon takes control of the kiss, grabbing the back of my head and angling me in such a way that he's able to deepen the kiss. I reach out a hand on his thigh to steady myself. My hand feels nothing but solid muscle.

What am I doing? Someone could see us at any moment now. Leaning back out of the kiss to put some space between us, Jaxon moves before I can utter a single word to him. The man grabs my hips and swings me over his lap so that I'm facing him. My dress rides up and I realize what I'm feeling is his hard cock directly against my hot center. Jaxon is looking directly at my breasts that have been conveniently thrust into his face. Throwing all caution to the wind, I run my hands through his short black hair, pulling softly so he looks up at me. This time, it's my turn to smirk.

"Like what you see, Jax?"

"Mmm, very much so, little sparrow. Do you like what you feel?"

I shift my hips, grinding down on his cock. He throws his head back, letting out a breathy moan before leaning back to my ear.

"Keep doing that and I won't be able to control myself."

The thought excites me and before I can stop myself, I grind down on him again, giving him a teasing smile and a flutter of my lashes.

I lean forward and whisper, "What if I don't want you to?"

"Don't make promises you can't keep, little sparrow."

In answer, I grind down on him and lean into his ear taking the lobe between my teeth and letting out a breathy moan. This man can have all of me. I might regret it in the morning, but right now, he has all of me if he wants it.

"Show me what you got, Jax."

Before I can even register what is happening, Jaxon lifts my hips and spins me around in his lap so my back is flush with his chest. His hands lightly feather up my thighs, pulling my dress up around my hips. I am a curvy woman, but Jaxon handles me like I'm light as a feather. Not wasting any time, he teases his fingers up my inner thigh and palms my throbbing center.

"Already so wet for me, aren't you, baby? Absolutely dripping in need for this cock."

I can't say anything. I'm desperate for something, anything this man can give me to soothe this aching need I have. He applies pressure with his palm on my clit, and I'm involuntarily grinding my hips back into him, desperate for some sort of release.

He lets out a low chuckle in my ear before taking his fingers and moving my panties to the side. He rubs my lips, teasing me with his slow perusal. I let out a breathy moan. "Jaxon."

"Hmm, little sparrow, do you want something?"

"Yes, please, yes. Anything," I reply, grinding my ass against his erection. I love that I'm affecting him as much as he's affecting me. I could get drunk off this feeling alone. Any moment someone could catch us, look a little too closely into our dark corner of the room. The thrill is intoxicating.

In answer, Jaxon takes a finger and slides it through my slick heat. I jerk, the sensation too much. He circles my clit in lazy circles before finally pushing a finger into my hot center, slightly curving his finger to find that sweet spot that has me riding his hand. As he fucks me with his finger, his thumb circles my clit at the same pace. He adds a second finger and I feel so deliciously stretched. His other hand comes up and wraps around my throat, squeezing the sides so the blood is restricted to my brain. The sensation is euphoric. He lets up slightly and the blood rushes back to my brain.

"Come for me, baby." I erupt around his fingers, the walls of my pussy squeezing him. He doesn't let up though, continuing to circle my clit at a grueling pace.

"It's too much, Jax, I can't." I back up against him, trying to escape his ministrations, but he clamps an arm around my waist, locking me in place.

"You can, and you will. You're going to take what I give you, is that understood?"

"Yes, oh god, yes," is all I manage to reply before I'm riding the next wave of orgasm as it rips through me.

FIFTEEN

JAXON

My little sparrow is so beautiful as she comes apart over my hand. Letting her come down from her back to back orgasms, I lightly brush my other hand up and down her arm, reaching up to her neck and massaging. She melts into me, leaning back against me. I move my hand around her and cup her breast. Teasing her nipple through her dress, I lean in and whisper, "You liked that baby? You're such a good girl, taking my fingers so well. Next time, it'll be my cock taking that pretty pussy."

She whispers my name when I praise her, relishing in the words of affirmation. She is a goddess and I am her god. She responds so well to me, every touch sending shivers down her body.

As I take my fingers from her heat, I gently command her, "Look. At. Me."

Once I have her attention, I take my fingers and suck them clean. I moan low in her ear. "Baby, you taste like sin and heaven." She visibly blushes and I move my hands down her body. Spreading my legs, I push hers together and pull down her dress from around her hips. I don't want anyone seeing that pretty pussy except for me.

She shifts against me, turning her body so that she's facing me. She lowers herself until she's on her knees. "Let me repay the favor?" she asks, looking up at me through her lashes. She runs her hands up my thighs and palms my cock through my pants. As much as I would give anything to have those pretty lips around my cock, I don't want to make her think she owes me anything. That's not what this is about. I could spend days worshiping her body and it wouldn't be enough.

"Maybe another time, little sparrow." I gently remove her hands but keep a hold of her wrists. I pull her up and pull her in for a kiss. Her lips are like pillows, so soft and pliable. She opens up to me, and I deepen the connection in a searing kiss.

Knowing my sister is probably going to come find Melody soon because it's getting late, I move Melody so that she's sitting next to me again. I place my arm around her and my other hand grabs her thigh possessively.

"Do you and my sister have a ride home?" I ask, knowing the only ride home she will be getting is with me.

"We're going to grab an Uber back to my place," she says, still flushed from a few minutes before.

"Let me tie up a few loose ends, and I'll give you both a ride home. Sound good?"

"Is this your sly way of seeing where I live?"

"Baby, if I wanted to take you home with sinful intent, it would be to my place, not yours."

"That's not what I meant," she huffs.

"I know it wasn't," I reply with a wink. "I just like getting a reaction out of you."

She rolls her eyes and it takes all of my restraint not to grab her by her hair and show her real sinful intent. I'd have her choking on my cock before she knew what hit her.

Before I do anything rash, I stand up and hold my hand out to her. "Let's go find my sister."

As we make our way through the crowd, we search for Brooke. I know she's safe as my brother has bouncers at each entrance, and they all have strict orders to never let her leave with an unknown man. A bit much, maybe. She is an adult after all. My brother, Kayden, is extremely protective of Brooke though and usually has an employee or two that also watch her whenever she's in the club. Some fuckers get inside that have no respect for women and would gladly steal what they want from them, so Kayden never takes any chances.

As we make our way through the dance floor, I catch movement in the corner of my eye. It's that douchebag from earlier that tried to grab Melody when they were dancing. He grabs Melody by the shoulder, turning her, and gets in her face. "Prude bitch. Thinks she's better than everyone else. Guess what bitch, you're nothing but a fat fuck anyway."

Melody looks taken back, tears gathering in her eyes. It takes me two seconds before I'm pulling Melody behind me and punching the fucker in the face, knocking him flat on his ass. The crowd collectively gasps and stands back, the music cuts off. The fucker has a nice cut on his cheek from my ring where I split him open. I reach down and grab the front of his shirt, getting real close so he can hear me. "She's mine, and if you value your life, you're going to apologize to her for what you said. Then you're going to apologize for touching what belongs to me."

Melody's eyes widen as I let out that last bit, and I have a feeling it will be a conversation later. Whatever. She is mine and the sooner she realizes it, the better.

"I'm s-s-sorry, man, I didn't know she was yours." He looks at Melody. "So s-sorry, I don't want any trouble." Before I can punch him again for lying, security comes over and grabs the guy under his arms and literally drags his ass out of the club.

Walking through the crowd, Kayden comes over and clasps a hand on my shoulder. "All good here, bro?"

"Yeah, Kayden, just some asshole that touched what wasn't his to touch."

Kayden looks over at Melody who is now so shocked her mouth hangs open.

"Nice to meet you, Melody," says Kayden, holding out his hand.

Schooling her features, she reaches out her hand. "Hi. It's a pleasure to meet you as well."

Kayden chuckles under his breath. "Anything I can get the two of you?"

"Nah, man, we're good," I reply. I know Kayden is probably itching to get back to whatever woman was probably sucking his cock.

"Alright, people, let's get back to the party," Kayden shouts and everyone starts to cheer. The DJ starts back up and it's like nothing ever happened.

I grab Melody's hand and continue to pull her through the crowd. I caught a glimpse of Brooke when all hell broke loose, so I make my way towards her location with Melody in tow.

Reaching Brooke on the second floor balcony, I tug Melody in front of me and circle my arms around her, placing my chin on her head. "Let's get you two home, huh?"

Brooke rolls her eyes. "Jax, you know there is only room for two in your car. Why don't you take Melody home, and when I'm done here I'll have Kayden bring me to her house."

Brooke looks at Melody with pleading eyes. She must have met someone tonight. Interesting. I look over at Melody to see what she wants to do. "Are you sure you'll be alright, Brooke?" she asks.

"Oh, I'll be fine. All the guys my brother hires always look after me. Don't worry, I won't be far behind you."

"Ok, if you think so." Melody reaches over and gives Brooke a hug. "I'll see you soon then. Be safe!"

"You too." She waggles her eyebrows at Melody before looking pointedly my way. I pretend I don't see the exchange.

"Alright, time for me to get Melody home. See ya tomorrow, lil sis. Don't forget we have family dinner tomorrow."

We wave bye to Brooke and make our way through the crowd once more. As we get to the entrance, I wave over the security and let them know we are ready to leave. He uses his earpiece to notify the valet that I'm ready to leave. It's nice having connections to the hottest club in the city. As we are waiting, I check my phone and notice ten missed calls from Franklin. *Why would he be calling so much?*

Melody looks at me with concern in her eyes. "Umm Jax, I think something is wrong. My alarm from the security system went off about an hour ago, and since then I've gotten alerts continuously."

I have a bad feeling about this. It's probably why Franklin was calling so much...

"It's OK. We'll head there right away." I grab her chin and make her look at me. "Everything is going to be OK, do you hear me? We will deal with this together."

"Thanks, Jax."

Once the security guard confirms the car has been brought up, he opens the door for us. "Have a nice night, Mr. Stonewell."

I open the door for Melody and guide her down into the bucket seat of my McLaren.

Time to get my little sparrow home and see what awaits us.

Sixteen

Melody

We zip through traffic and I notice the way that Jaxon drives like he's a professional, zig zagging around cars effortlessly. Oddly enough, I don't feel unsafe. It comes as a surprise. Maybe it's because I'm so trusting of this man before me or that I know he would never intentionally hurt me, but whatever it is, I can't get enough of it. It's addicting.

As we round the corner to my street, the night is illuminated with red and blue flashing lights. Dread sinks into my stomach. *What happened now?* We pull to a stop in my driveway; the only clear spot to park with all the police vehicles everywhere. We exit the car and are immediately greeted by a sheriff who, judging by his appearance, may be in his late fifties and probably close to retirement.

"Good evening, young lady. Are you Melody Harper?"

"Yes, this is my house. What's going on?"

"Well, someone tripped the alarm in your place. The inside has been ripped to shreds. I have to ask, is there anyone that would want to hurt you?"

"Well... I was attacked last year in Silicon Valley. They never caught the guy. It's honestly the only person that I could imagine that would want to harm me."

"Interesting... when did this attack happen?" he asks, taking notes in his notepad that he removed from his uniform pocket.

I give a look at Jaxon and he must get the hint because he moves back over to his car and leans against it. I'm not sure I'm ready for Jaxon to look at me any differently once he finds out what happened. I'm falling for this man, and I'm scared.

"It was June sixteenth of last year. My friends and I were out bar hopping. When I left the bar to catch my Uber, I was attacked and... raped."

"Alright, ma'am, I understand this might be difficult for you to recount. Let's save you the trouble and I'll just have one of my officers pull up the report from the incident, okay?"

"I would be very grateful for that, thank you."

The sheriff goes off to talk to one of his officers, and I make my way back over to Jaxon. His jaw clenches and he looks ready to kill someone. Fuck, he probably overheard what I told the officer.

I look up at him sheepishly, not sure what to say. I find that words aren't necessary though as Jaxon pulls me into him and wraps his arms around me. It's the first time in forever since I've been held like this, and I can't help but to melt into his arms. Tears spring to my eyes, but I blink them back. I can't lose my composure just yet.

"Thank you," I mumble into Jaxon's chest. His only response is to squeeze me a little tighter. I am in deep trouble with this man. If he keeps it up, he'll own my whole heart.

We wait outside for what feels like an hour before the sheriff comes back over.

"Well, Miss Harper, we have documented all there is to in the house and took statements from your neighbors that heard the commotion. You're free to go into the house, though I warn you, it's a disaster. You probably need to spend a lot of time replacing things. And make sure to get your security system replaced."

I swallow the lump in my throat and simply nod at the officer and offer him my thanks. Jaxon puts an arm around my shoulder and leads the way into the house. The police lights slowly disappear as everyone leaves the crime scene.

As we make our way in through the garage, the mud room and kitchen seem fine. *Maybe the officer exaggerated it a bit?*

I'm soon met with an obscene amount of damage in the living room. My couch cushions are completely slashed open, the curtains are hanging in tatters, and lamps and decor lay shattered on the floor. My hand flies to my mouth as I stare in disbelief. *Why would someone do this?*

With trepidation, I turn and make my way up the stairs. There is a slash along the wall leading up the stairs, as though whoever did it had a knife dug into the wall and dragged it all the way up. Chills run down my spine. *What if I had been home?* Would my body be mutilated to pieces right now?

Jaxon follows me up the stairs. Once I get to my room, I gasp. My bed is completely untouched, but there are what looks like blood splatters all over the walls and my dresser mirror. I walk farther into the room and see that my bed isn't completely untouched like I thought. In the center of my bed lies a single white rose with splatters of red. The contrast is significant against the red background of my comforter.

I look over at Jaxon to see him clenching his fists. He looks like he wants to murder someone.

"We'll catch whoever did this, Melody. Mark my words," he all but growls to me.

I'm exhausted and probably coming down from the adrenaline running through my veins. Jaxon must see my exhaustion because he puts an arm around me and says, "Why don't we go to my place for the night. I'll send Brooke a text to head back home, and we'll worry about her car in the morning."

As I start to refuse his offer, he levels me with a glare. "There is no way you're staying here tonight. Not with this psycho on the loose, no working security system, and nothing to protect yourself."

I'm about to tell him about the gun in my nightstand, but

before I can utter a single word, he's leading me back down through the house to his car. Running on autopilot, I get in the car willingly. He's right... as much as I don't want to admit it, I can't stay here tonight. *What if he comes back to finish what he started?*

The ride passes in a blur. Jaxon keeps one hand on my thigh the entire way, lightly rubbing my skin with his thumb. It's so relaxing, I soon find myself lulling off to sleep.

"MELODY, BABY, WAKE UP." SOMEONE IS JOSTLING ME awake. I look up through half lidded eyes and finally become aware of my surroundings. It's just Jax. We must have finally got to his house, except now that I'm looking around, we seem to be in some sort of parking garage.

"Where are we, Jax?"

"This is my parking garage. We will have to take the elevator to get to my suite."

"You live in a penthouse suite?!"

"Yes, little sparrow, I do."

Jaxon removes his seatbelt and then rushes out of the car to get my door. As I stand, I'm completely unsteady. The events of the night come rushing back to me, and soon I'm hyperventilating. *I can't believe this is really happening...* The parking garage starts to spin, and the last thing I hear before everything goes black is Jaxon. "Melody, are you ok?"

I come to and realize I'm laid out on a sleek black leather couch. There is a fan above my head slowly spinning, casting a cool breeze on my skin. There's something cold on my forehead; I reach up and discover a wet rag.

Footsteps sound from somewhere in the house, and eventually Jaxon comes in to view. He changed down into gray sweats and a fitted white T-shirt. He looks delectable. Whoever said gray sweats do something for a man, wasn't lying. Jaxon sees me stir awake and comes right over, sinking down to his knees at my side.

"You gave me quite the scare, little sparrow."

"Sorry, Jaxon. I don't know what happened. How did you get me up here?"

"You fainted, I caught you just in time before your head hit the cold concrete. And I carried you up here in the elevator, of course."

My skin heats under his perusal. I'm definitely not a light girl. I'm instantly embarrassed that he had to carry my weight up here. "Sorry you had to do that, it probably wasn't easy."

He grabs my chin and forces me to look at him. "Don't you dare start insinuating anything about your weight. I love every curve on this body. I'll show you how easy it is."

Jaxon stands up and hooks an arm under my legs and an arm behind my back before he picks me up. I let out a little squeal, imagining him dropping me to the ground. But what he does next surprises me. Not only does he lift me up, but he takes me down the hall and we enter a dark room. Jaxon flips the light and I'm looking at the biggest master suite I have ever seen, with a panorama view of the city lights below.

Jaxon turns a corner and brings us to a bathroom, where he sets me down. He lowers the toilet lid and moves me to sit down on it. He kneels down and ever so slowly lifts up my right foot to delicately remove my high heel. He places my foot down and does the same with the other. He looks up at me through his lashes. "You do something to me, Melody. I am completely enthralled by you."

My skin flushes. This man has a way with words. I reach over to him and pull him up to me. My small hands frame his face and I lean in and place a kiss upon his lips. It quickly turns to molten heat as the kiss consumes us both. Jax stands, taking me with him, not once breaking the kiss. He spins me around and pins me against the wall. One hand is restraining my hands above my head, and the other one wraps lightly around my throat. The pressure he places on each side of my neck is exquisite, and soon I'm panting with pure need for this man.

"Hang on, little sparrow." He breaks the kiss. "Let's get you cleaned up first."

Confused at what he means by that, I give him a questioning look. He turns to the walk-in shower that takes up half of his bathroom and turns on the hot water. His shower is grand, that's for sure. It has a rainfall nozzle overhead and jet sprays coming from the two side walls. It looks like heaven, but I hope he isn't expecting me to get naked in there with him.

"Melody, I can see your gears turning. Stop it right now." He moves to lift my dress over my head and I swat his hand away.

"I don't want you to see me naked just yet."

"Little sparrow, I told you. I love every inch of this body."

"It's not that Jax... it's just... I was in a dark place a year ago. I still wear the scars from that dark part of my life," I admit, looking down at the ground.

He puts a finger under my chin, tilting my face up to look into his blue eyes.

"I said all of your body is beautiful, not just parts. All of you is a masterpiece to me."

"Where are they," he asks, reaching out a hand to me.

"My wrists and lower arms..."

"Let me see, Melody. Let me see every beautiful inch of you." He slowly reaches down to the hem of my dress and begins to pull it up. I bite my lip.

"Hey, what did I say about biting your lip, little sparrow? I only have so much restraint, and right now I'm trying to be gentle with you."

I quickly release my lip and give him a small smile. He continues to lift the dress until it's over my stomach. I reach up my arms so he can fully pull it off. The cold air brushes my skin and I break out in goosebumps. All I'm left in is a bra and a thong panty.

Jaxon takes a step back and admires me as I am. "God, you are beautiful, Melody. I don't care how many times I have to say it until you believe it, but you are absolutely breathtaking."

I have no words for his admission, so I do the only thing I can think of. I start to take off my bra and pull down my panties, stepping out of them before placing them on my dress.

"Fuck, Melody... you're absolutely perfect." He steps forward and grabs my arm, peppering light kisses up over my scars and repeats the process with my other arm.

Although his appraisal turns me on, I'm not sure I have the energy for whatever he has in mind right about now. At least if the bulge in his sweatpants is anything to go by.

"Melody, what I wouldn't give to push you against this shower wall and fuck you senseless, but I know you are not ready for that right now. Let's take a shower and get cleaned up, then we can head to bed. It's been a long night."

Relieved, but also slightly disappointed, I nod my head and step into the shower and let the hot water sink into my bones. I watch Jaxon as he gets undressed. I was right when I saw his picture on Tinder. He is loaded with tattoos. I wonder if any of them have a special meaning... I take a moment to appreciate his physique. He reaches down to pull off his sweats and then he's just in his boxer briefs. The man is sin personified. He stalks toward the shower, stopping only to take off the last barrier. He sheds his boxer briefs and if I thought he was impressive through his clothing, it has nothing on how big he actually is.

"Keep staring, Melody, and I'll have you on your knees with my cock buried so far down your throat you won't be able to breathe."

I look up to meet his eyes so quickly, he lets loose a small laugh. I quickly move aside so he can join me in the shower. The room quickly steams up and it's just the two of us in this world. He looks over to me tenderly, reaching behind my head for something. He comes back with a loofah and soap. Before I can get a word out, he lathers it up and starts washing my body. He starts with my arms, then my shoulders, working his way around my neck. He turns me around so he can get my back, and then he's reaching around me and bringing the loofah across my sensitive nipples. I gasp at the sensation and look over my shoulder, giving him a glare. He puts his hands up in mock surrender.

Laughing to myself, I take the loofah from him and finish washing myself. The soap is a manly scent, but I don't even care. As long as I get to be surrounded by this man's smell, I am A-OK with it. Jaxon takes the loofah when I'm done and washes his body. We both make quick work of our hair and face. Even being completely cleaned, I still feel filthy thinking back to that night. I usually am pretty successful with pushing those thoughts away, but with the events that occurred at my house, I'm struggling to ignore it.

Jaxon must sense my inner turmoil because he comes up behind me and wraps his arms around me, placing a gentle kiss on the top of my head. I wish I could stay here forever.

Once the water starts getting cold, we both turn off the nozzles and get toweled off. Jaxon lends me a pair of his boxer briefs and a T-shirt. Both freshly dressed, Jaxon leads me back to his bedroom. I still can't get over the view. It's amazing. I never thought I would be a big inner city girl, but it's beautiful. I can imagine watching the sun setting here every single night.

WHOA girl. Ok, slow down. I am getting too attached to this man too fast. What is it about him that has me so entranced?

Shaking myself out of my reverie, I see that Jaxon is waiting expectantly at the edge of the bed. When he sees that he has my attention, he holds out a hand and pulls me to him.

"Little sparrow, what are you thinking in that pretty head of yours?"

"Just that you're wickedly handsome and attempting to steal my heart."

"I don't make attempts, Melody. I meant it when I told you I get what I want."

I let out a little huff. He can be so infuriating. But isn't that part of what I like about him, his possessiveness? He said it at the club, I belong to him. I think most girls would be pissed at that statement, maybe even call it a red flag; for me, it's a fucking turn on.

Jaxon smirks at me. It's like he can read my mind and knows I'm falling fast for him.

"Let's lay down, little sparrow. It's getting late and I know you're exhausted."

Climbing over him, I get comfortable in the bed and settle in. Before I can even get a "goodnight" out, I'm being pulled across the bed. Jaxon envelopes me in his arms, and I've never felt safer.

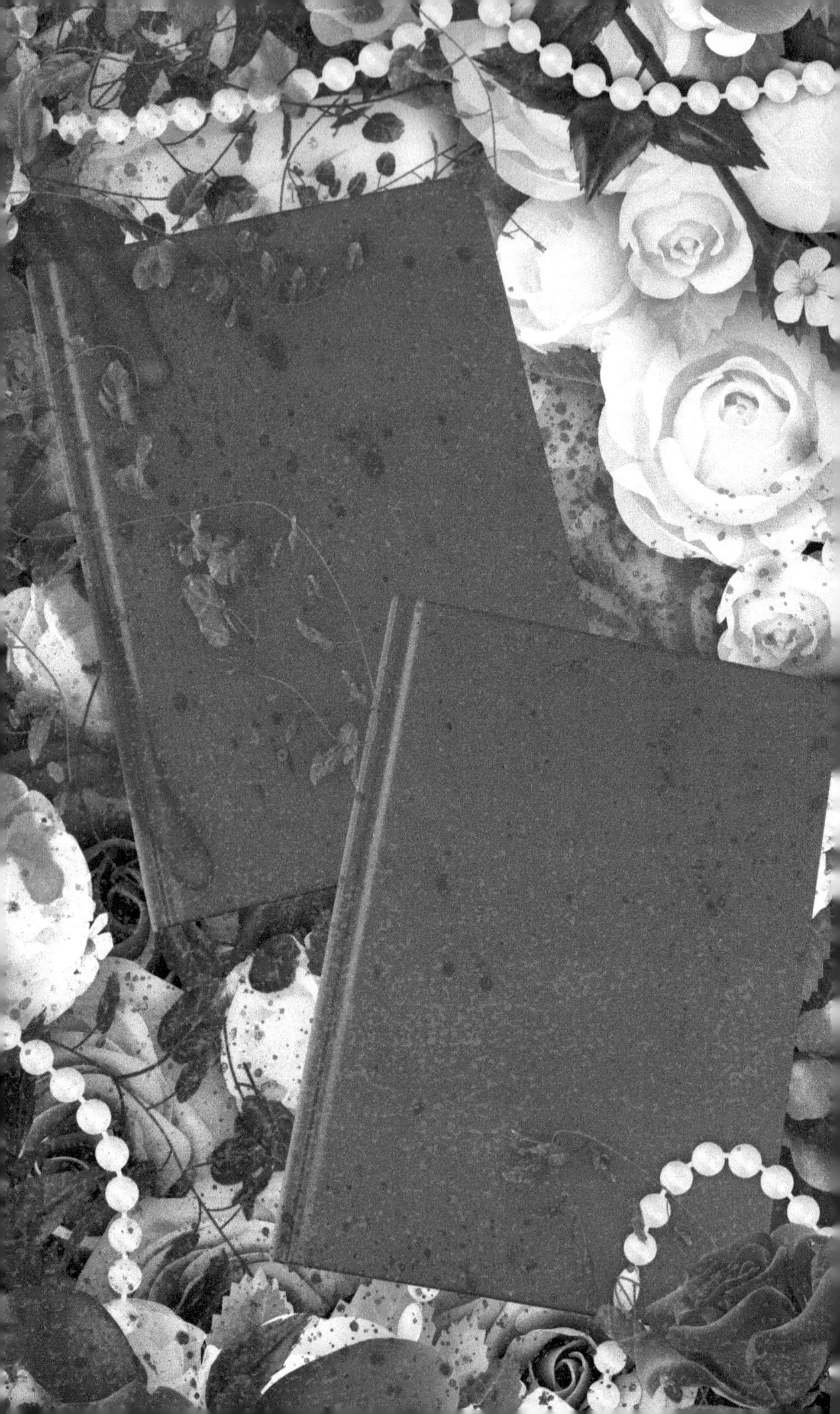

SEVENTEEN
MELODY

All I hear is beeping and people talking, but I can't make out what they're saying. The air has a clean, sterile smell to it. I try to open my eyes but they feel so heavy, *everything* feels so heavy. It hurts to take too deep of breaths so I try to focus on evening out my breathing. I keep fighting to get my eyes opened, and finally I manage a small peak. The tiny action hurts and it doesn't seem like my other eye is opening. I take a look at my surroundings but everything is so blurry.

"Hi there, hunny, how ya feeling," asks someone behind me somewhere. I try to get words out but my throat is so dry. "Oh dear, here let me get you a water."

I prop myself up a little bit while she's gone, careful not to pull out my IV. She comes back shortly after with a cup of water with a straw and holds it up to my mouth so I can take a sip. I've concluded at this point that I'm in a hospital, but I don't remember why. Everything is so foggy. The only thing I remember is being out with the girls bar hopping.

"Sweetie, the doctor will be in shortly. Try to get some rest until he's here, OK?"

"Where are my parents? Has Brian visited?"

"Oh that must have been that handsome fellow that came by earlier this morning. He left that beautiful white rose on your table. Your parents just left a bit ago to get some rest. It's five in the morning after all, dear."

"How long have I been here?"

"Well, you've been here two days already. Your parents have been taking turns coming to see you."

Her words shock me. Two days? *What in the hell happened to me...*

The nurse leaves and I lay down on the bed. I must doze off, because I'm startled awake by a knocking on the door. "Come in," I say hoarsely. I reach over for the water and take a few more sips.

"Good morning, Miss Harper. I'm very impressed that you are awake so soon."

"Am I not supposed to be?"

"Well with the... injuries... you sustained, I would have expected the swelling in your brain to take a few more days to subside. Now, that doesn't mean we aren't happy you're awake. Everyone heals differently, and in your case, you're a fighter."

"What injuries did I sustain?"

"Well, you had a broken nose and a zygomatic fracture, which is just a fancy term for a broken cheekbone; that is stable and non-displaced. There was also blunt force trauma to the back of your head resulting in a skull fracture. Now the skull fracture wasn't so serious that we needed to do any surgical repairs, thank goodness, but it'll heal on its own after a while. It did cause some brain swelling, which is why you have been out for the last two days. You have numerous cuts and bruises all over your body, and significant bruising on your neck and ribs, which is why your throat probably feels very raspy right now and your sides ache..."

He starts to trail off, and I ask the next, more daunting question.

"What happened? I have no recollection past my girlfriends and I bar hopping."

"Well, to put it bluntly, you were attacked, Miss Harper. Quite brutally if I might add. You had the date rape drug in your system, and from what I have been told, some people leaving the bar heard someone moaning, in apparent pain, in the alley. The good samaritans entered the alley to see what it may be, and that's when they found your body.

"Now, I want to be very honest with you, Miss Harper. We had to do a rape kit on you. According to witnesses, it was very obvious that you had been sexually assaulted."

Is this what shock feels like? A ringing in my ears, all other sounds slowly being drowned out, while my vision, or what little I have, starts tunneling and soon there's nothing at all.

I vaguely feel someone shaking my shoulder and saying my name, but it feels so far away.

"Miss Harper, can you hear me? Miss Harper! Stephanie, please fetch our recovery kit, and bring her an apple juice as quickly as you can. Now, please."

Everything comes back at warp speed and it all feels too loud. Memories come rushing back to me, and I wince, remembering the most brutal parts. This can't be happening... I can't... What if I'm pregnant? *Oh my god*... I'm slowly falling apart at the seams. I feel so incredibly dirty, like I need a hundred showers and to scrub myself clean a thousand times.

I close my eyes and try to stop the panicking. Just as I'm coming back to myself, I hear a gasp in the doorway and in walks my dad. That's when the tears let loose. I've always been a daddy's girl and this time is no different. My dad rushes over and gives me a kiss on the head.

"Hi, pumpkin, you had us scared there for a bit, didn't ya?"

"Dad, I'm so sorry..."

"What in the hell are you apologizing for, Melody? None of this is your fault."

"Yeah but if I wasn't out with the girls, or maybe if I hadn't left my drink unattended... maybe things would have been different..." I trail off knowing I sound ridiculous but also not wanting to come under my dad's scrutiny.

"Pumpkin, the police officer probably hasn't been by yet, but there's a good chance that even if you weren't drinking, that something would have happened. They think this guy had been following you for more than a few hours. I don't know all the details, but apparently your car was broken into earlier that night. They lifted a partial print from your door handle that matched a partial print from your handbag at the scene of the attack."

"I'm not saying it's right, but I just thank god he didn't kill you... that you're still here with us."

I understand what he's trying to say, but in reality, a part of me did die that night. I feel it now in my very soul. A part of myself that I may never get back. I had been saving myself for mine and Brian's wedding night, now that's been taken from me, too. *Oh god, what is Brian going to think?*

"Dad, does Brian know what happened?"

"He was here when the police filled us in, yes, but honey... He came by the first night, but since then we haven't seen him. He mentioned something about being busy with training... I'm sorry, pumpkin."

My dad visits for a while longer, but leaves once the police officer shows up to ask me some questions. I tell them all I know, which isn't much honestly. The officer elaborates on the events of that night, stating someone probably put the date rape drug in my water, but they don't think it was my attacker.

They let me know that my attacker scraped and cleaned my nails before he left, washing away any trace of him I might have been able to get from the damage I inflicted on his arms. Great, that means I crossed paths with two people that night who came with horrible intentions.

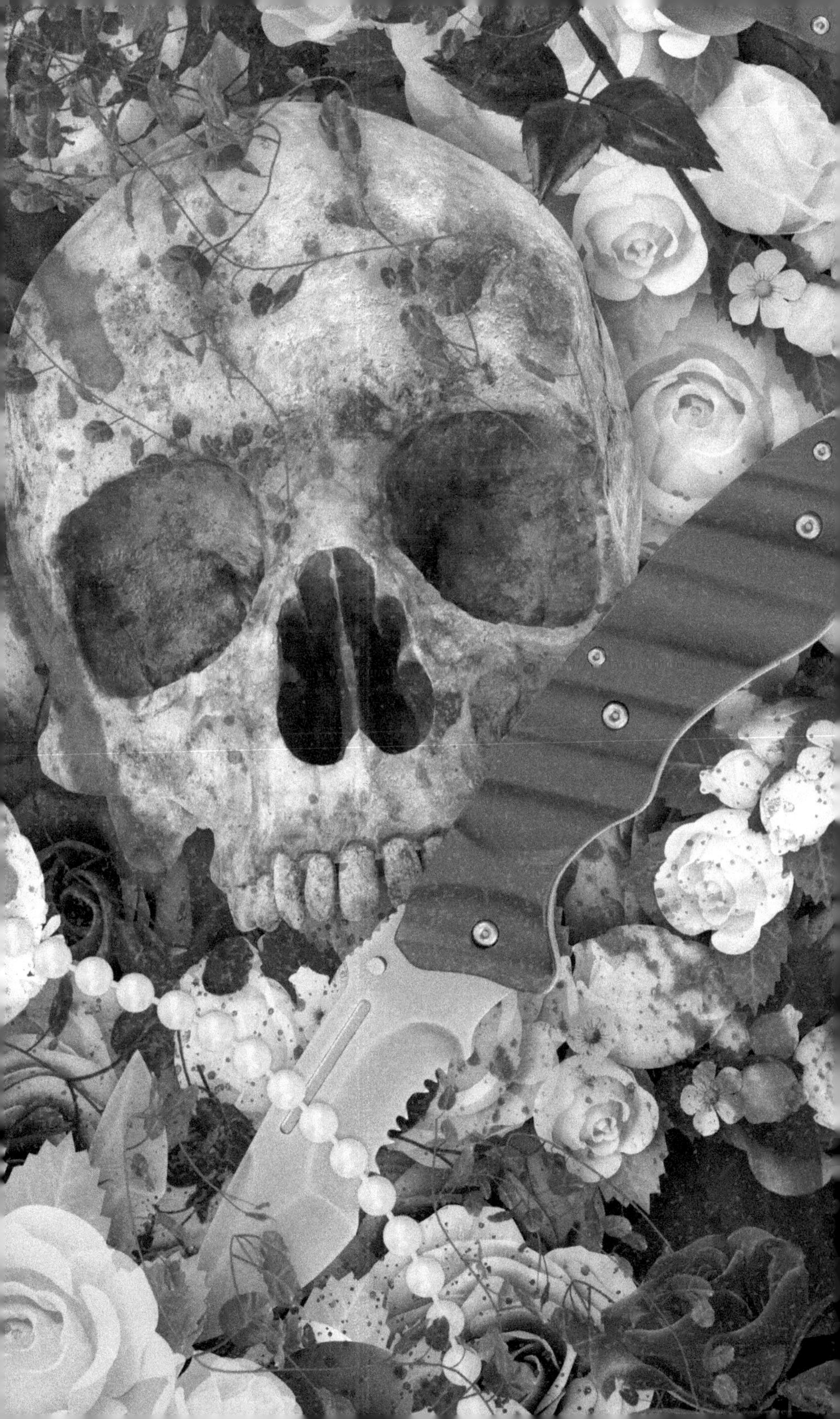

CHAPTER 17.5
UNKNOWN

PRESENT DAY

I may have gone a little overboard with my knife tonight, but I think the message was received loud and clear. I was going to have so much fun with Mel tonight, but that was quickly ruined when I entered her house to find her nowhere in sight. Mel has been a homebody for this entire past year, why is she suddenly changing her routine?

Mel did show up later with the guy that's been following her. That had my vision turning red again. To ease my anger, I went out and found another woman, one who looked just enough like Mel. I took everything she had to give, imaging it was Mel the entire time. Eventually though, I saw through my own delusions and was disgusted. It was always the same, no one ever compared to Mel. I choked the life out of the little slut before dumping her body in the river that runs through the city.

Maybe another day, Mel. Maybe another day.

Eighteen

Jaxon

Present Day

I lie awake and watch Melody sleep. Her eyebrows are furrowed like she's thinking really hard, and every now and then she lets out a little mewl. Thinking she must be having a bad dream, I rub soothing circles on her arm. I could lie here forever if it meant she was the one I was holding.

Even her smell, vanilla and berries, is strong enough to peek through my body wash from our shower and has me addicted. I don't think I could ever get too much of my little sparrow. I breathe in her scent and hold it in, squeezing her to me just a little tighter. This is where Melody belongs. Here in my arms.

From texting every day to our meeting at the club, everything seems like it's happened so fast, but also not fast enough for me. I want Melody's whole self, her love and her affection. The sooner she realizes she is mine, the better. Though, she never corrected me when I told that douche at the club that she belonged to me. Maybe my little sparrow is already starting to see how good we are together, how much I already own her body and mind.

I'll be damned if she changes her mind at this point. The thought makes me growl with need to claim what is mine. No one will take her from me, not even herself. I'll make her mine if I have to, in any way I have to. The only thought in my mind right now is putting my cock in her and marking her as mine in every way possible.

My growing erection says exactly what I want to do to her right now. Running my hand down her arm, I bring my hand to the edge of the boxer briefs I let her wear and slip my hand inside. I grab a fistful of her ass and can't help but to grind into her, pulling her body flush with my cock. Before I can make any other moves, Melody is jolting awake, a scream dying on her lips, and breathing rapidly. I reach up a hand to her shoulder and try to calm her down the best I can. "Shhh, little sparrow, it was just a bad dream."

"Oh my god, Jax, you have no idea..." She turns to me and buries her head in my chest. As her breathing starts to slow, I continue rubbing my thumb along the bare skin on her back.

Even in her vulnerable state, all I can think about is burying my cock so far into her pussy that she no longer remembers her dream, let alone that anyone else exists except for me and my cock.

"What can I do, Melody?" As my hand moves to tangle into her hair, I pull back and angle her head so I can kiss her deeply, claiming her with my tongue.

She pulls back. "I don't know, Jax, you're doing a pretty good job as it is."

Needing no further prompting, I push Melody down and bring myself over her, settling in between her legs. My cock is right there... how easy it would be to undo those briefs and just let myself slide right into her slick heat. I have to control myself though. When I put my cock in her it'll be because she's begging for it like her life depends on it. Melody lifts a brow at me... oh she wants to be a brat this morning does she?

"Take off the shirt, Melody."

She listens so perfectly that my cock strains against my briefs, dying to bury myself into her slick heat.

I bend down and take her lip between my teeth, pulling and biting just enough to cause a sliver of pain before I'm claiming her mouth, dancing my tongue with hers. As I brace myself on one elbow, I take my other hand out of her hair and gently run it down her creamy throat, briefly pausing to squeeze the sides ever so slightly before continuing my perusal further down her chest, until I get to the underside of her breast. Cupping her soft flesh, I break the kiss and bring my mouth down, licking a slow path to her nipple. I take the bud into my mouth, sucking and licking. Melody is panting beneath me, grabbing my hair and causing a bit of pain. The pain is delicious and lets me know exactly what Melody needs right now.

I take her nipple between my teeth and give it a quick bite, just enough to have Melody arching her back off the bed and a small hiss to leave her clenched teeth. My little sparrow enjoys a little bit of pain too.

Giving her other breast the same attention, I move my hand lower, over her soft stomach and down to her pussy, slipping two fingers into her slick heat. "So wet for me aren't you, little sparrow?"

Removing my hand from her briefs, I look up at Melody and slowly bring my fingers to my mouth, sucking her very essence from my fingers. She tastes like heaven.

Melody watches me with hooded eyes. When I suck her clean off my fingers her mouth pops open with slight surprise. "Mmm, Melody, you truly taste divine. Now let me show you just how much I enjoy the taste of you."

Lifting myself off her body and sitting back, I grab the briefs at her waist and slowly peel them down her body. I remove one leg from the confines, then the other, until she's spread before me like a Thanksgiving meal. My little sparrow is all soft curves that I just barely restrain myself from biting into.

Lowering myself so my breath fans her pussy, I lift one leg at a time over my shoulders.

"Jax, I don't know..."

"Hasn't a man ever worshiped you with their tongue, little sparrow?"

"Actually, no," she says while propping herself up on her elbows, looking down at me sheepishly.

I all but growl at her admission. It turns me on that I will be the first to give her this experience, but also pisses me off that she's never been taken care of.

"Well, little sparrow, let me just show you what you've been missing." I push her back down into the pillows and bring my mouth back over her pussy.

Taking her lip between my teeth, I give a slight bite before gently pulling. I give the same attention to her other lip. Lightly, I take my tongue and slip it between her folds, running the length of it through her wetness, from bottom to the top. I circle her clit with the tip of my tongue before giving it a flick that has Melody pulling my hair and arching off the bed.

"Mmm, you like that, huh, little sparrow?"

Focusing back on her clit, I become a ravenous man, circling and licking her with abandon. As my tongue gives her clit all the attention, I take a finger and push into her. Melody moans with the intrusion, but she doesn't stop. She clenches around my finger and I start to move it in and out, slightly curving my finger to hit that sweet spot that I know she loves so much. At the same time, I start sucking and biting her clit, just enough to cause her some pain before licking it away.

"Take what you need Melody, I'm all yours." Melody needs no further convincing. She pulls my hair to hold my head exactly where she wants me and she rides my face, taking everything she needs.

"Right there, Jax, oh god..."

Sensing she must be right on the edge, ready to tip over, I reach my other hand up and tease her nipple. The combined sensations push Melody over the edge and she's coming. I lap up all that she gives me, continuing to move my fingers in and out of her, letting her ride the waves of her orgasm. Her pussy clenches around my fingers and her clit throbs against my tongue.

This woman is going to be the death of me. This deadly desire I have for her knows no bounds. I would do anything for her. I'm fucking falling, and I don't care if I don't make it out alive. She is my salvation. She is everything to me. I fucking love this woman.

The thought takes me by surprise for a moment before I'm full on accepting my fate. I knew I was obsessed with her and have this need to make her mine, but I can say I love this woman with all honesty.

She owns every broken piece of my heart and every blackened bit of my soul.

NINETEEN
MELODY

I've never had a man use his tongue on me like this. Brian and I were always saving ourselves for our wedding night.

Jaxon circles my clit lazily which is slowly getting me needy again. Before I fall too far into the sensations, I pull on his hair until he's looking up at me through his lashes.

"Yes, little sparrow?"

"Jaxon, please, I need you." Not even sure what I need or what I'm asking for, I pull his hair one more time before he obliges and makes his way up my body. I can feel his erection against my thigh, and it's making me even more wet.

Before I can say anything, Jaxon leans himself on one elbow, and uses his other hand to guide his cock through my wetness. The feel of him brushing through my wet folds has my back arching from the bed, and I'm wiggling to get more friction. I'm desperate for him and he knows it.

"What can I do for you, little sparrow? What do you need?"

It's like he wants me to beg for it.

"Jaxon, please…"

He brings the head of his cock to my clit, circling it with slight pressure.

"Please what, little sparrow? What does my girl need?"

"That right there... please, Jax."

"You're going to have to be more clear... use your words, little sparrow. What. Do. You. Need?"

"I need your cock, right now, please," I beg him. I literally beg him to take me.

"Fuuuuck, that's my good girl."

Before I can put two thoughts together, Jaxon lines up his cock to my slick entrance, and in agonizingly slow torture, pushes his cock into me inch by inch.

I am being stretched to the delicious point of pain, and I don't know how much more of him I can take. Peeking down, my eyes widen in horror. Oh my god, he's only halfway in... This man is going to split me open.

Jaxon looks up at me and smirks. This crazy man must be reading my mind, because he stops. Completely stops.

"Ready for me, little sparrow?"

I nod my head and in a move so fast I'm still processing it, he pulls out and flips me over on my stomach. Kneeling behind me, he grabs my hips and pulls me up to him. My face is down in the mattress, so I turn slightly to look at him over my shoulder.

"I'm just enjoying the view, Melody," he says, slowly stroking his cock. "One day, I'll take this hole too." At first I'm confused, and then it hits me when he takes a thumb and applies pressure to my tight hole. I shriek and clench my ass cheeks. There is no way anyone is putting anything in that hole.

"Jaxon!" I exclaim. Jaxon chuckles low before gripping my hips again. He reaches over me, arching his body over mine and teases my breast. The action makes my nipple rub on the sheet and it's the hottest fucking thing.

"Melody... are you ready for me baby?"

"Yes, please. God, yes."

Gripping my hip with one hand, Jaxon takes his other hand and guides his cock to my entrance. Pushing in so just the tip of him is in, he stops. "Last time, baby, are you sure you want this?"

"Jaxon, god dammit. Yes, please, I need you."

Jaxon thrusts into my soul so hard I'm seeing stars. He pulls out slowly, then slams in again to the hilt. Taking one of my legs, he moves it over his hip, and all of a sudden this new angle has him buried even further at his next thrust. It feels so goddamn good. We get in a rhythm, and as much as he's thrusting into me, I'm thrusting back onto him.

"Jaxon, oh god, I'm so close."

"Come apart for me, little sparrow." I reach a hand down and find my clit. As he thrusts in and out of me, I circle my clit, riding his dick and my hand at the same time.

"Come for me, baby." As though my body is connected to his every command, my body clenches around his cock and I'm falling into oblivion. I moan out, encouraging Jaxon to come with me.

Jaxon ups his pace, relentlessly pounding into me. Just as I'm not sure I can take anymore, Jaxon pulls out and hot spurts of cum land on my back and ass crack.

"Sorry, little sparrow, wasn't sure if you have any kind of birth control or not."

Letting a small laugh slip past my lips, I assure him. "I'm on birth control. No worries for next time."

"My little sparrow is so confident there will be a next time..."

"There better be. I need a mind blowing orgasm like that every day," I reply.

Jax chuckles before moving to get up. I look up at him questionably, wondering what he's doing now. "Just going to get a wet rag, little sparrow."

When Jaxon returns with the wet rag, he wipes me clean, peppering kisses along my spine. Although we most definitely just fucked, his aftercare is so tender. I feel another splinter of my heart being owned by this man before me. I don't know how long until he owns it completely, but I feel as though it's close. He looks at me with—dare I say—love in his eyes, and I'm free falling into their silvery blue depths.

I'm falling for this man, hard... and it won't be long until he owns me in every way possible.

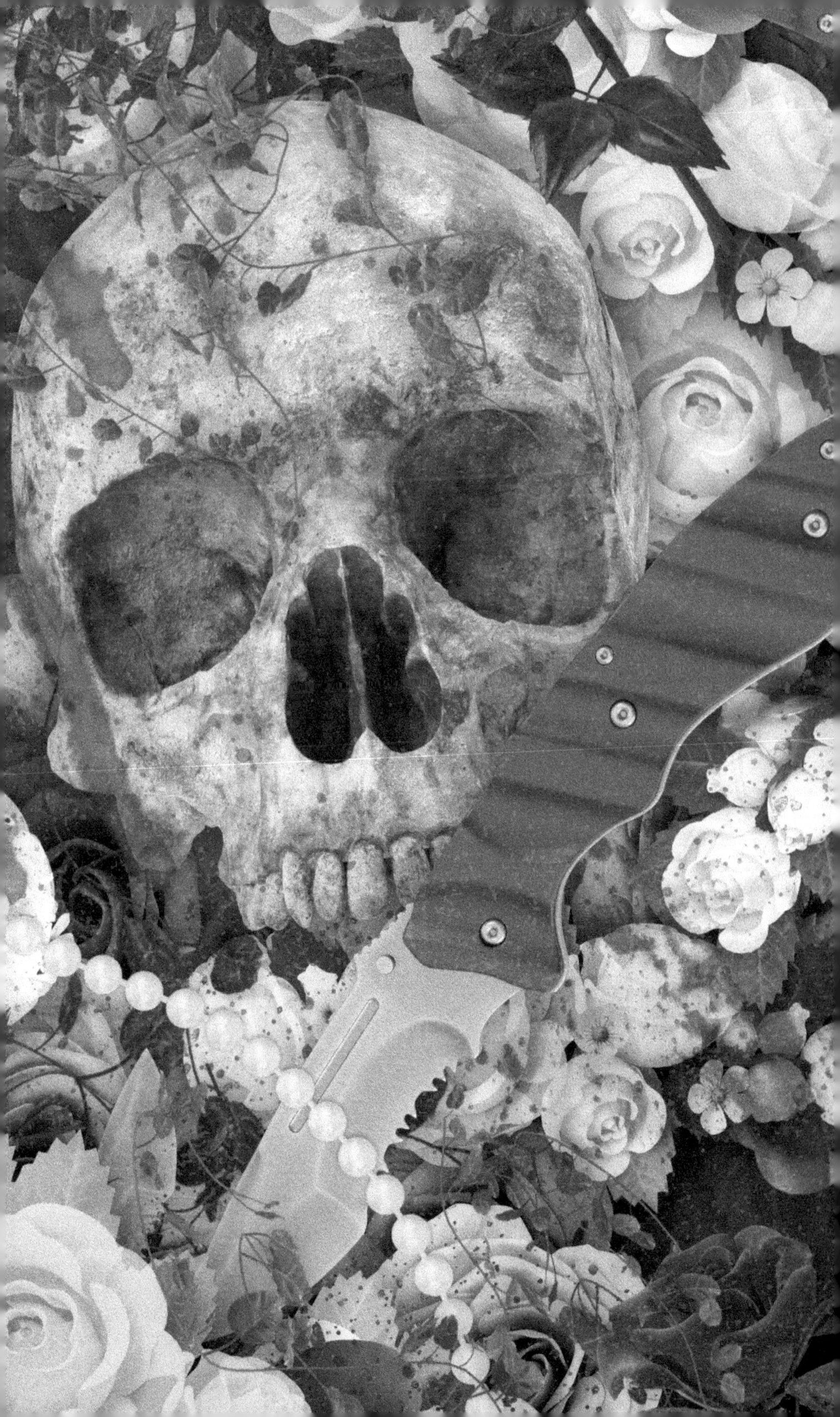

Twenty

Jaxon

Melody has all of my heart. Every single fractured piece, she absolutely owns me.

I take care of my little sparrow, wiping her clean. After tossing the rag into my clothes basket I lie back down with her. She has her arms folded under the pillow as she lies on her stomach, her head turned towards me.

"What are you thinking, little bird?"

"Just that your tenderness is always at war with your rough exterior. And I mean that in the most delectable way possible."

"I would be anything for you. Rough, tender, degrading, praising, you name it baby, and I'll be that for you."

Melody lets out a soft, contented sigh. She looks beautiful in my bed, the sunlight washing over her skin casting a soft glow.

"I know you would be, and that scares me."

"Why does that scare you, little sparrow?"

"Because I'm afraid there will be nothing left of my heart to give to you, you'll own it completely."

"That shouldn't scare you baby. If your heart is mine, I'll protect it with everything I am."

Melody closes her eyes and lets out a small breath.

"Jaxon... please don't break it. I don't think I could survive it if you did."

Melody admitting her heart is mine makes my chest clench with love. I love my little sparrow, and although Melody didn't say it outright, I know that she loves me too.

"Also, Jax... umm... Thanks for being gentle with me for my first time... Well, at least my first consensual time. I don't talk about it much—well, with anyone. But he stole everything from me, Jax. Everything," she says, her breath catching.

My heart simmers with rage but also swells with pride at being her first. I refuse to even acknowledge what that fucker did to her as her first actual time.

I take Melody's face in my hands and gently kiss the tip of her nose. "Of course, baby. Anything you need, but just so you know, I'm not letting him steal anything else. He can't steal this from us, this is ours." I motion between us.

"Thanks, Jax, for everything," she says with a wink, the playfulness coming back into her eyes.

"Well, little sparrow," I say, tucking a strand of hair behind her ear, "I can promise that the next time we do this, I won't be so gentle with you. But the best part is that you'll be begging for more."

"Ohh really?"

"Yep. The next time I take that pussy, it's going to be so rough you'll be seeing stars."

"Jax," she all but moans.

"Nope, none of that, little sparrow. I'm going to go make us some breakfast. Relax, go to sleep, whatever you need to do, but let me do this for you."

"Ok, Jax. I'll wait here," she replies, tugging the blankets around her so she's completely cocooned in warmth. "I'm always so cold," she says sheepishly.

"Good thing I run hot." I wink at her, coaxing a chuckle from her beautiful mouth.

As I make breakfast, I shoot over a text to Franklin. I never got the opportunity to call him back last night so hopefully he fills me in today. Not even ten seconds later and Franklin is texting me back.

FRANKLIN

Bro, what the fuck?

Is Melody OK?

ME

Yeah man, she's fine.

I brought her home with me last night. We crashed at my place.

FRANKLIN

Well, I have a video clip that I need you to watch.

It's pretty graphic, so maybe make sure Melody isn't around.

ME

Alright Franklin, just send it over.

Melody is still in bed, so I have time.

I click on the video play button and I'm met with an image of Melody's bedroom. The time in the bottom right of the video shows 8:54 P.M., right around the time that I caught sight of Melody at the club last night.

A masked man enters her room from the doorway to the left, slowly looking left, then right. Chills break out over my body. He has a large knife, holding it loosely at his side. Suddenly, he roars, plunging the knife into the door. He stabs multiple times with rage that is so apparent it radiates off his very being. The guy is beyond pissed, probably because Melody isn't home like he was planning. I hate to think what he had planned with a knife that big. Dread settles low in my stomach while rage is boiling my blood.

Panting heavily, evident by the way his shoulders are heaving, he walks farther into the room, surveying the landscape. He then exits the screen to the left as he enters her walk-in closet. When he comes back out, he's looking down at something in his hands. Getting close to the screen, I can see that what he holds is the pearl necklace. He slowly lifts his head and looks directly at the camera. He tilts his head to the side and makes his way slowly before he's standing beneath the camera, as though he's looking directly into my soul.

"Hello, Melody… we were supposed to have a little fun tonight. Though, I guess now it'll just be me that has a bit of fun."

His voice sounds distorted like he's talking through a voice scrambler of some sort. He makes his way to the bed and grabs something out of his pocket. Before I realize what is happening, the guy is releasing his erect cock from his pants and slipping on a condom. He wraps the pearls around his hand and starts to stroke himself with them.

He turns to look at the camera. "Like what you see, Mel? You make me so uncontrollable. I can't even think clearly when I smell you all around me, much like in 305."

Less than a minute and the fucking guy releases his load into the condom, panting and resting his chin on his chest. He takes off the condom, ties it, and pockets it in his jacket before tucking his limp dick back into his pants and zipping them up. Poor guy is a two pump chump, that's for sure. Reaching into a different pocket inside his jacket, he brings out and places a white rose on her bed.

He walks slowly back to the camera, tilting his head right,

then left. He reaches up to the camera as though he would grab a neck and brings the camera close to his mask.

"Melody, Melody, Melody... You and I are going to have a lot of fun the next time I see you. I hope you're looking forward to it, like the dirty whore you are."

"I'll be seeing you again soon, Mel. But not soon enough"

At this point, the feed cuts and there's nothing but blackness.

"What. The. Fuck," I say out loud under my breath.

This guy is certifiably insane, and well, smart. He left no DNA at the crime scene and wore thick leather gloves. He somehow found out where she lives when he originally brought the pearls to her house. He seems to know a lot about how to leave a clean crime scene, both a year ago and even now. I start to wonder if we can use that information to get closer to finding out who this is. Maybe someone from her school that also studied criminal law?

ME

That's some of the most fucked up shit I've ever watched. Give me a bit to think on it, I might have to do some digging with Melody. It really seems like whoever this is, knows her well.

Can we look into her social media for anything suspicious from her friends list? Maybe someone from school?

FRANKLIN

I'm sayin... yeah man, I'll do some digging.

ME

Thanks for sending me this man.

Hey, can you also hire some of Kayden's guys to do a complete gut and replace on Melody's place? They will need to do some cleaning of the walls in her bedroom, too.

FRANKLIN

Absolutely. Will do.

I'll let you know once they're finished.
Probably around 3-4pm.

ME

One more thing Franklin, I'm sorry, but can you pick up some clothes for Melody? I'll transfer you money for it.

FRANKLIN

Sure thing. Just send me over her sizes.

After sending him her sizes, I set my phone down and I finally finish cooking up the bacon and pancakes. Slathering the pancakes in butter and syrup and setting the bacon on the plate, I bring Melody breakfast in bed.

When I walk into the bedroom, Melody is already sitting back against the pillows, with the blanket wrapped around her chest. She instantly smiles when she sees me, and god damn if my heart doesn't stutter at the pure beauty of it.

"How did you know?" she asks sweetly.

"How did I know what?" I ask her back.

"That I like my pancakes smothered in butter and syrup. Most people don't put enough on them."

"I just know you that well, little sparrow."

Melody eats her meal in silence, though I keep catching her stealing little glances at me.

"What's the matter, baby?"

"Just enjoying the view I get with my breakfast."

"Is that so..." I guess I can understand that. I am in nothing but boxer briefs after all.

I reach across the bed and grab the back of her head, bringing her in for a kiss. My girl tastes like syrupy goodness, and I'm a starved man.

We spend the rest of the morning exploring each other's bodies and talking about everything under the sun.

I learn even more about Melody than I knew before, and everything I learn just solidifies the amazing woman I knew she was. If I thought there was any chance of me not falling even more in love with this woman, those chances just flew out the window. I'm thoroughly and completely in love with my little sparrow.

TWENTY-ONE
MELODY

I am completely screwed. I thought maybe I'd learn something about Jaxon that would have me taking a step back with my feelings, but turns out I'm just falling for him even more.

He and Brooke were orphaned at a young age when their parents had a horrible car accident. Their Aunt Jenny and Uncle Bill took them in and became a bonus set of parents for them. They had also adopted James and Kayden a few years before.

Once Brooke and Jaxon turned eighteen, they both came into a lot—and I mean *A LOT*—of money. The first thing Jaxon did with his was buy his aunt and uncle a bigger home. Though, they did keep it modest according to Jaxon. He said they've always loved to live simply and refused to take any bigger of a house than what he got them.

Jaxon took the rest of his money and invested it. With the help of Franklin and James, he was able to quickly multiply his money a hundred times over. According to numerous articles, he was one of the fastest growing billionaires in California. Even though he's rich-rich, he still donates to and attends different charity events throughout the year, and actually has one coming up that he would like me to attend with him. It surprises me I haven't seen him at charity events before; my parents used to love parading me around at them in hopes of finding someone to marry me off to.

I was surprised when I learned just how rich he is. He definitely doesn't act like he's rich and too good for everyone. Which just makes me fall for him a little bit more.

Needing to finally burst our little bubble of perfect happiness, I mention to Jax that it's probably about time that we head back to my place to start the cleaning process.

"Already taking care of that, little sparrow. They should be finished by early afternoon, if you want to head there afterwards?"

How is this man even real? From mind blowing orgasms, to cooking me breakfast in bed, to now taking care of my home. I swear this man's love language is acts of service, because does he ever love to serve.

I look at Jax and can't help the little laugh that slips out. "You are something else, you know that? Most women would think you are a walking red flag, with your possessiveness and take charge attitude. Honestly, all it does is turn me on."

Jaxon levels me with a heated look. "Don't talk about being turned on unless you plan on acting on it, little sparrow."

"Hmm, but I can't help it, I'm already so wet," I tease him.

Quicker than a fox, Jaxon has me on his lap, my ass in the air and briefs pulled down, and a slap ringing out around us.

I'm so confused by what just happened, all I do is lay there with my mouth open.

"I told you Melody, I take what I want." Another slap lands on my already red ass. The pain is biting, but then he rubs the pain away. The process repeats itself for five more rounds. By the end of it, I'm left panting and absolutely soaked.

"Jax, please."

SLAP. SLAP. SLAP.

Three quick slaps to my ass and I'm crying out with each one.

"What did I tell you about using your words, little sparrow. Tell me what you want or so help me god..."

"Jax... I want... I want to go to your office. I've been a bad girl."

It's Jaxon's turn to look shocked. With a smirk and without wasting any more time, Jax leads me down the hall into his office.

MAKING MY WAY AROUND THE DESK, I MAKE A MOTION with my hand for Jax to have a seat. We are both still wearing his boxer briefs, except he's shirtless and I'm in a white tee.

As Jax takes a seat, I take off my shirt, letting the cold air pebble my breasts. Jax hisses as he intakes air at my sudden strip show. Feeling confident, I walk over to him and lean over to his ear. "Do you like what you see?"

He simply nods. Next, I turn and place my back to Jax, slowly taking off the boxer briefs. With them in a puddle at my feet, I step out of them and make my way back over to Jax. I straddle him in the chair, nothing but his own briefs between us. I can feel his erection against my stomach, and it takes everything in me not to remove it from his briefs and simply *impale* myself on it.

Running my hands through his hair, I yank back his head and kiss him. We are a clash of teeth and tongues as passion consumes us, but this time I'm in charge.

I back out of the kiss, moving to Jaxon's neck where I suck and lick a path down his chest and over his stomach. The muscles there ripple with each kiss I place on his tanned skin, until I make my way lower.

Grabbing the top of his briefs in each hand, I tell him, "Lift your hips for me, Jax."

I make quick work of removing his briefs, where his erection bobs right in my face.

Taking his length in my hand, I begin to lick him starting from the bottom and making my way to the top, before circling his head with my tongue. I take him into my mouth, sucking and licking like it's the greatest damn lollipop I've ever had.

Looking up at Jax through my lashes, I can see him throwing his head back in the chair and his hands clenching the seat.

Needing no further prodding, I take the length of him all the way to the back of my throat. My eyes start to water but I fight the need to gag. I hollow out my cheeks and suck and lick on him like my life depends on it.

"Holy fuck, Melody. Such a good girl, taking every inch of me."

I look up at him through my lashes and am greeted with a lust fueled gaze.

"Look at you, choking on my cock like my good little slut."

His words of praise only spur me on. I pull his cock out of my mouth with a pop.

"Do you like that baby?" I ask him as I continue to stroke him with my hand. I need to hear him say it.

"Fuck... yes..."

Taking him back in my mouth, I grab his cock and jerk him off while sucking and licking with my tongue. Using my free hand, I cup and massage his balls.

His hands fly to my head, grabbing a fistful of hair. The pull causes pain, but it's a delicious sort of pain. "Melody, I'm going to come..."

Taking it only as a challenge, I take him down my throat like his good little slut. Swirling my tongue on the underside of his cock, he starts thrusting into my mouth, fucking my face. As I feel his balls tighten in my hand, and his thrusts become jerky, I increase the pressure and I suck him as he comes, swallowing everything he gives me.

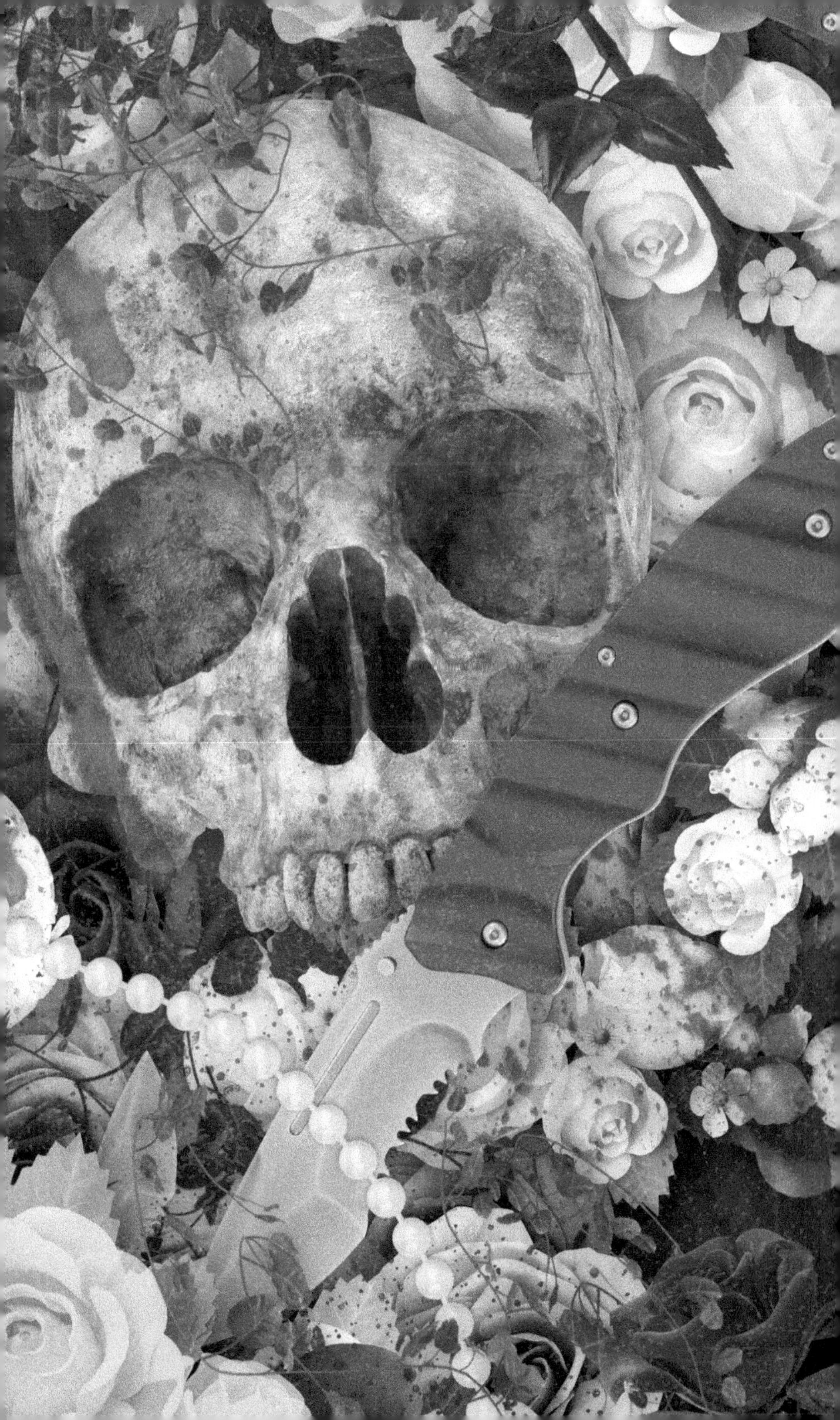

08:45

Twenty-Two

Jaxon

Holy fuck... Melody has a mouth on her. As she pops my cock out of her mouth, she smirks up at me. "Was that good baby?"

"You have no idea, little sparrow. I knew getting those pretty lips wrapped around my cock would be the most pleasurable sin, but baby, I was not prepared for that."

She gets up before me and goes back to straddling me in the chair.

"What should we do with our day, Jax?"

I playfully grab her ass. "I can think of a thing or two... ok fine, just kidding. Wanna go for a drive? Afterwards, we can stop at your place and check it out."

"That sounds like a good idea."

As Melody heads to the bedroom, I take the elevator down to my delivery box. I knew Franklin wouldn't let me down. There is a bag with jeans, a shirt, a pair of converse shoes, a new bra, and panties. The possessive side of me is clenching my jaw knowing that Franklin knows what Melody is wearing under her clothes, but I assure myself it was necessary to get what she needed. At the bottom of the bag are toiletries and feminine products, along with lavender scented shampoo and conditioner, and makeup, of all things.

Franklin really thought of everything. At the bottom of my delivery box sits something unexpected though. A single white rose lies crumpled at the bottom, red splatters on the petals. Just like the one on Melody's bed.

I take a good look around, instantly feeling on edge. That fucker knows where I live now. This is getting out of hand.

Seething with irritation, I head back up to my suite. I lay the crumpled rose on the dining room table before heading into the bedroom to find Melody.

What I find stops me in my tracks. Melody is wrapped in a sheet, staring out into the city. Her silhouette against the city background is stunning. As I walk up to her, I set the bag of items on the bed and then wrap my arms around her.

She leans her head back into my chest and I just hold her. I know she has been through a lot this past week, but she is so incredibly resilient.

"I'm so proud of you, little sparrow."

"Oh yeah? Why's that?"

"Your strength just amazes me. You're not letting this fucker win, and it's awe inspiring."

"I learned after my attack that I couldn't let him prevent me from living. I went through a period of time where I didn't know how much longer I would be alive, Jax. That changes a person. I've come out stronger, and I did it on my own. I fought tooth and nail for it, but I did it. I won't let him take that from me now."

My little sparrow is a sight to behold when she shines in her strength. Giving her one last squeeze, I turn around and head back to the bed. Grabbing the bag, I hold it out for her.

"Everything is in here that you could possibly need, courtesy of Franklin. He may or may not have had the guys fixing your house look at what makeup and feminine products you use so he could buy you the same exact stuff. There is a drawer free for you to use on the right hand side of the double sink in my bathroom, please feel free to put your stuff on the counter and in the drawer."

"Jax, we should talk about this..."

"No, Melody. It's not up for discussion. Until this guy is caught you're staying here. There is no possible way that I'm letting you out of my sight. This guy is crazy."

"But what about what I just said. I won't let him ruin my life."

"Staying with me is not ruining your life, little sparrow. Look at it as a vacation. I already paid Brooke to cover your position indefinitely, and we can check on your house everyday if you want. But I would feel better if you stayed here with me. No one is getting into my suite."

"Hmph... I'll think about it, Jax."

"You'll think about it, but it doesn't change the decision I've already made."

Leaving the bathroom to let Melody get ready, I head into my closet to get dressed. Now that she will be staying here, we will either have to get her items from her house or buy her new things. Melody doesn't seem the type to accept an entire free wardrobe, so picking up her clothes from her house makes the most sense. I have more than enough room in this walk-in closet for her things, too.

Picking out a pair of jeans and a fitted black T-shirt, along with my own Chuck Taylor's, I quickly get dressed and freshened up. Knowing that we are going to be doing a bit of driving today, I picked comfortable clothes instead of my usual polished attire.

Once Melody is ready, we head down the hall to the elevator. As we pass the dining table, Melody freezes.

"Jax... what is that doing on the table?"

I stall for a second wishing I had just thrown it away and avoided worrying her.

"It was in my delivery box today when I went to grab your things."

"Jax... that means he knows where you live. What if he tries to hurt you? I could never live with myself..."

I stop Melody and place both of my hands on her shoulders. I peer down at her until she looks into my eyes. "Melody, don't spiral on me. We are OK. Look at me. Nothing is going to happen to me, little sparrow."

Melody's lip quivers as she tries to hold back tears. "But... Jax..."

"But nothing, Melody. Let's go enjoy our day. Like you said, let's not allow this fucker to ruin our lives."

"Ok," she says, voice trembling.

We go to the elevator and make our way to my garage. I let Melody pick between the McLaren and the Ducati.

"I don't know if I'm ready for a motorcycle ride just yet... let's take your McLaren."

As I hold the door for Melody to get into the car, I send a quick text to Franklin letting him know about the rose in my delivery box. Franklin insists he never saw it when he dropped off Melody's things, but then again, he didn't actually look in the box before placing the bag in there.

Knowing that this fucker is toying with us now, my very being is completely on edge and on high alert. It's why I decide to conceal carry my H&K USP Compact .45. It carries ten rounds plus one in the chamber, and I have an extra magazine in the car for emergencies, so I am definitely prepared should this fucker try anything.

With us both settled into the car, I start her up and let her purr to life. After waiting a few minutes for the idle to settle, we exit the garage and start driving to nowhere in particular.

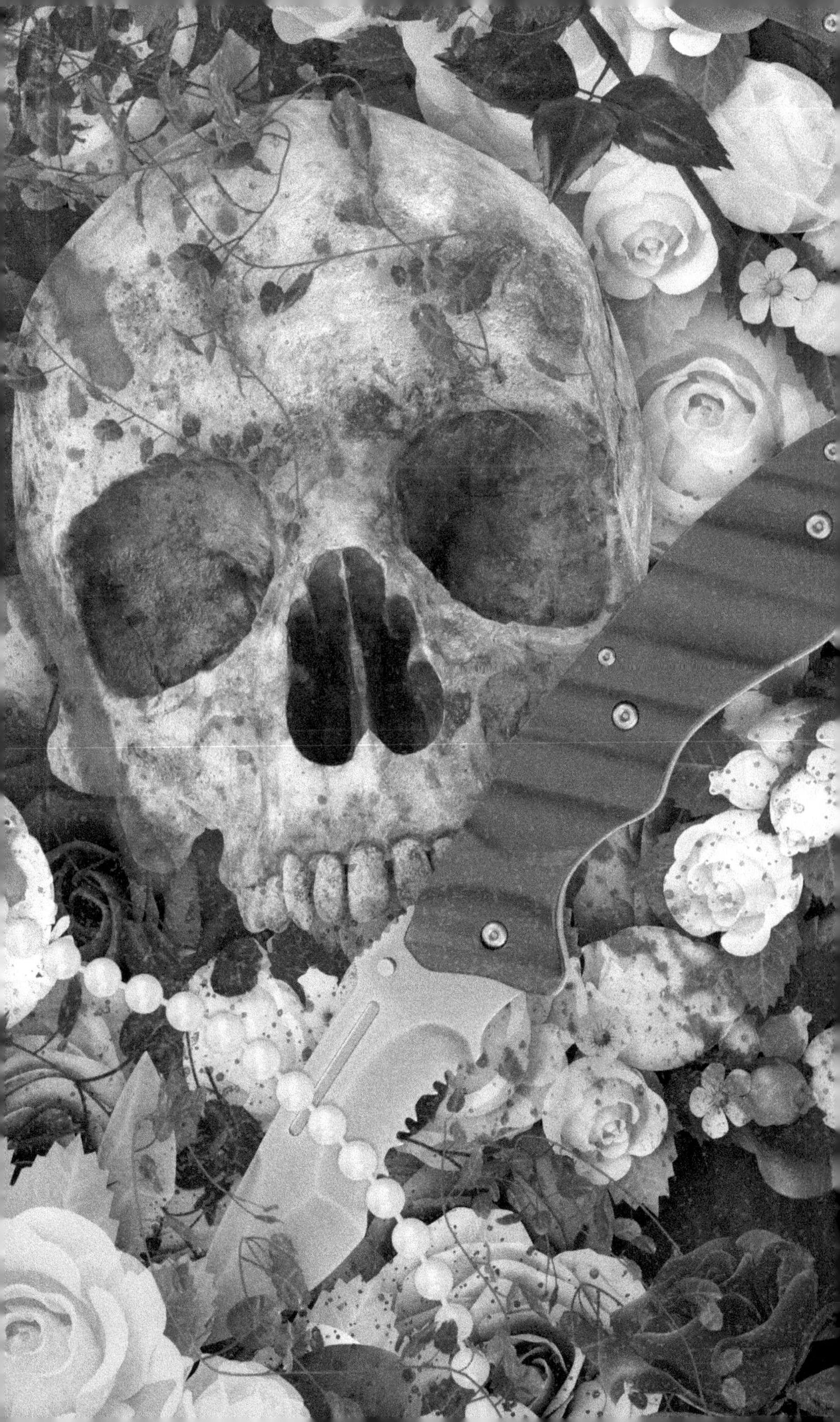

TWENTY-THREE
MELODY

Jaxon takes me on numerous scenic routes, some I never even knew existed. It's all so beautiful though; the west coast of California is breathtaking this time of year.

As we cruise through the surrounding area, Jaxon takes me to his Aunt and Uncle's house to pay them a quick visit.

Jaxon introduces me as his girlfriend and I'm blushing from the title he has bestowed upon me. I suppose what we are, most would consider a serious relationship, but we haven't had that discussion yet. Just something else I'll need to ask him about in the car.

We sit and chat with them for a bit, before we take off again. We stop in a few small towns with the cutest downtown areas and do a little shopping. I pick out a few new items of clothing to keep at Jaxon's place and a new hoodie to keep me warm on those chillier spring nights. We stop at a boutique on the town's main street and I pick out some lingerie too. Jax is all too excited for me to try them on when we get back to his place.

Around 2 P.M. we stop and have a late lunch at one of the ocean side restaurants lining the coast. Jaxon orders the surf and turf while I order a grilled red snapper with mango poppy seed sauce. We talk more about our lives growing up and I still insist we must have met at some point. I learn that we attended similar charity events in the past, but I suppose there *are* usually so many people there it's possible we just never ran into each other. *Like we just weren't meant to meet yet.* As Brooke would say, it was probably divine intervention.

I really am starting to believe Brooke on that though. Everything has fallen into place since meeting Jax, other than this fucker trying to come back into my life. It just feels right. I don't know how else to explain it. He would seriously be considered a walking red flag to most women, but I have always seen red as a pretty shade of pink anyway. Plus, he's so god damn mouth watering and possessive to the point he makes me undeniably wet. He's thoughtful and always ready to do and be whatever I need.

Once we're ready to go, Jaxon picks up the bill and we decide to head back to my place. It's about an hour to get there, so I pull my kindle out of my purse and start reading while Jax drives.

The hour drive to my house feels like only twenty minutes have passed as uneasiness settles into my stomach. What if he's in there? What if he comes back for me? Jax senses the change in me and puts a hand on my thigh. "You ok, little sparrow?"

"Yeah, just freaking out a bit."

"It'll be OK. We'll go in, survey the work they did, grab a few things, and then be gone. In and out, no problem."

Only, we don't get in and get out. Not because of anything to do with my attacker, but because we argue about the work done in my house. They did an amazing job, the house looks like nothing ever happened. Everything that was shredded or broken has been replaced with the same or similar items. It's quite impressive really. But what doesn't sit right with me is that yet again, the Stonewell family has paid for everything.

"I am not a charity case, Jax. I can pay for things myself."

"With what money? Your mom and dad's? No, I take care of you now. Anything you need, I will provide."

"I have money set aside, Jax. Money I received when I turned eighteen, much like yourself. Though it's nowhere near the amount you got, it's enough to pay for the repairs."

"Little sparrow, we're not having this argument anymore. It's done and there's nothing you can do about it now."

"Jax, this isn't right... this is not how a relationship works."

"Oh... let's talk about that last bit. We ARE in a relationship Melody, one where I provide for you. Whatever you need or want. It's my job to see that you get whatever your heart desires."

"Ugh, Jax. We're in a relationship, huh? Are we officially putting titles on each other, because at your Aunt and Uncle's house you were quick to call me your girlfriend even though we never talked about that."

"Yes, little sparrow, you are my girlfriend. If I had the choice, you would be my wife, but seeing as I can't convince you to go off and get married to me right this second, I will settle for 'girl-friend.' For now."

My mouth hangs open at his audacity. *His wife?! Oh my god, we have only been whatever this is, for a week.* I stomp off to my closet to grab a few pairs of underwear and my favorite bras. Stuffing them in a bag harder than necessary, I grab my perfume as well and stick it in the bag. Seeing that Jax's car only has room for the two of us, and has almost non-existent trunk space, I lay out the clothes I want to bring to his house on my bed. He assures me that his men will grab the clothes tomorrow and bring them to his house, along with the shoes I picked out.

Exiting my bedroom, I yell down the stairs to Jax that I am ready to go. He appears at the bottom of the stairs, waiting for me to descend. He doesn't say anything, but he wears a cocky smirk on his face like he's won. I suppose he has as I'm willingly going back with him.

The car ride is essentially silent as we both focus on our own thoughts. I'm still upset at him for paying for everything without talking to me first. He's probably over there simmering that I'm not his wife right now. Whatever the case, he still has one hand on my thigh, and while I'm upset with him, I still feel comforted by that small presence.

As we get close to town, we start to run into a bit more traffic. The light turns green and Jax takes off. Before we make it halfway through the intersection, I turn to see lights coming at us before they're slamming into Jaxon's driver side, the screech of metal and tires filling my ears.

We must be spinning through the air because I see glass fall past my face to the roof of the car before coming back down again. I'm slammed side to side before the vehicle comes to a stop. As I come to, I feel a trickle of blood running down my face, but the world is filled with smoke and sirens.

I look over and see Jax is completely knocked out. I reach out my hand to his neck, hoping to god that there is a pulse. Panic overtakes me when I don't immediately find one, however I push down a little more and feel the steady thrum of his pulse. Before I can even exhale a sigh of release, my passenger side door is being yanked open, my seatbelt undone, and I'm being dragged away from the vehicle. I look back to see a masked man and dread fills me. Now that I'm out of the car, I can see it is slightly on fire, and I have renewed panic that Jax is still in the vehicle.

"JAXON!" I scream with everything I have. I see him stir slightly before his head slumps down again.

"JAXON!" I scream again before something is put over my nose and mouth. I breathe in something sweet and cloying before my world starts to darken. The last image I see before I pass out is Jax lifting his head and struggling to get out. He won't be able to though, he's pinned.

It's the last thought I have before my world goes completely dark.

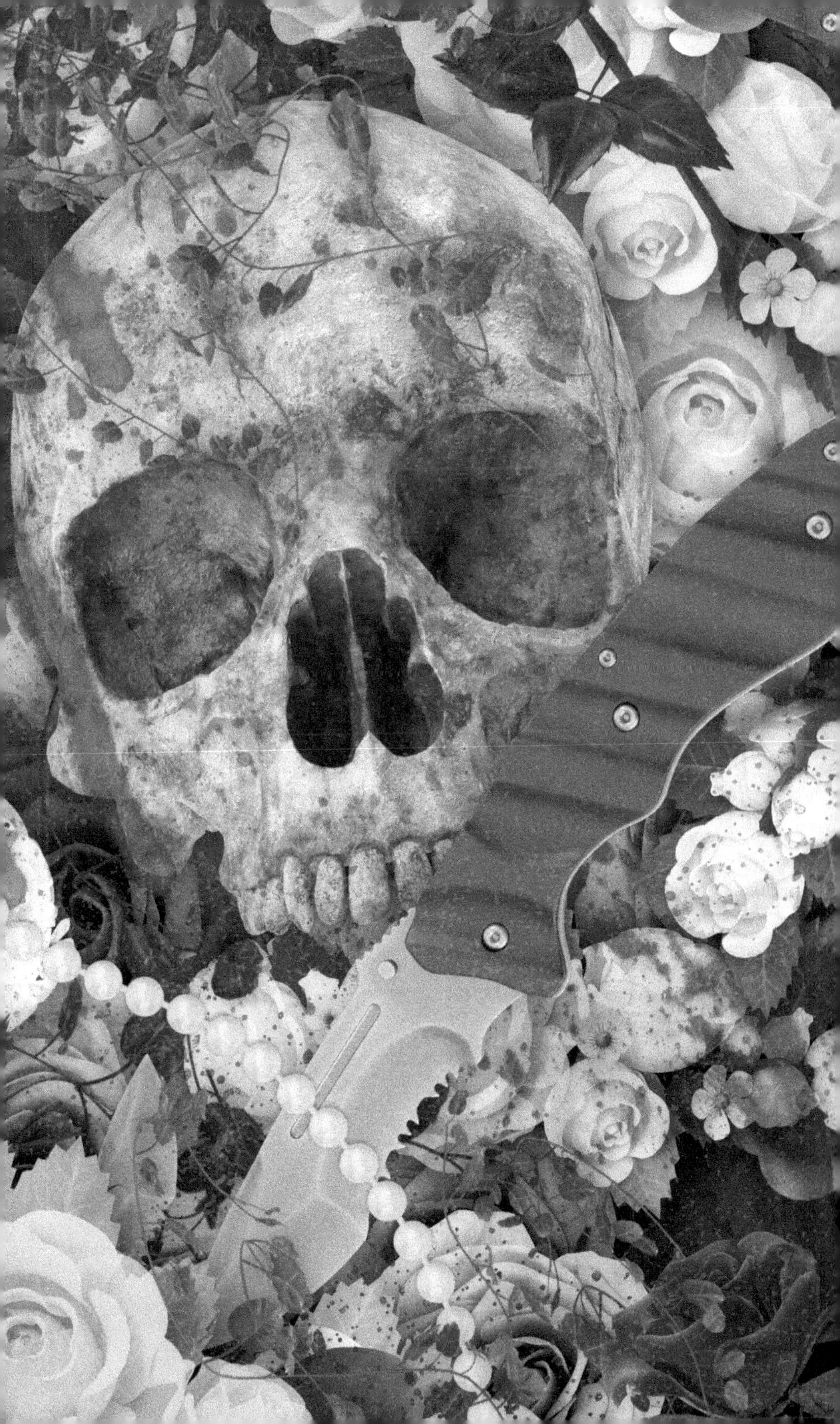

08:45

Twenty-Four

Jaxon

"JAXON!" I hear Melody scream, but everything is so heavy I can barely lift my head. I'm out of it and can barely think straight. I smell smoke and burning rubber. I try to move my hand over to the passenger seat to check on Melody, but my hand meets nothing but air.

My eyes snap open. Where is Melody?

"JAXON!"

My head whips to the sound of her scream, only to see a masked man placing something over her mouth and nose. She looks at me once more before her eyes close and her whole body slumps in his grasp.

"MELODY!" I scream, my voice hoarse from all the smoke spilling into the car.

He takes her, before I can even try to get out of the car, he takes her. My world starts to spin and it's only then that I notice a chunk of metal sticking out of my abdomen, blood quickly pooling through my shirt and soaking my jeans. I tilt my head back against the headrest, trying to find the strength to fight the impending darkness, but it's no use.

I succumb to the darkness with Melody's name dying on my lips.

THERE ARE PEOPLE TALKING IN HUSHED WHISPERS around my bed. I can't make out who it is, but at the mention of Melody's name I'm stirring. The events that landed me here come rushing back, and I'm sitting up so fast I have a sudden ripping pain in my stomach, and I scream out.

"Whoa whoa, Jax, calm down," says Franklin to my left. "Page the nurse," he says to someone I can't see just yet.

"I already did the moment his heart rate accelerated." It's none other than my brother, James. I'm relieved that he's here, he'll know what to do, how to fix this.

"But he took her, Franklin. She's gone." I'm barely holding it together, tears are streaming down my face just remembering the terror on Melody's face. I couldn't protect her when she needed it the most.

"Jax, we know. We have all our men looking for her. So far we haven't turned up anything, but we aren't giving up," says James.

"How long have I been out for?"

"It's been four days..."

"WHAT?! He's had her for four days?" At this point I start ripping out my IV line and start undoing my gown.

"Jax, you need to wait, you're bleeding. You probably ripped open your stitches," pleads Franklin.

James puts his arms on my shoulders and gently pushes me back down on the bed. "He's right, you know. There is nothing you can do right now except get better so that we can all put our heads together to find her."

"You guys have no idea the torture she could be going through right now."

They both look at me with pity in their eyes and a look of defeat. Not defeat like they are giving up at finding her, but defeat at realizing I speak the truth. Who even knows the horrors Melody has been going through for four fucking days.

"I've been combing through the class list from her graduation, but I'm not turning up anything, Jax. I'll keep looking but it might be a dead end," says Franklin, trailing off.

"No... no... I won't accept that. We're missing something, it's at the edge of my mind, but I don't have a fuckin' clue what it is."

"I definitely feel like this is someone that knows her on a personal level of some sort. We just need to make a connection. The dots are there, it's up to us to connect them the right way," replies James, ever the level headed one of the bunch.

The nurse comes into the room rather hastily and exclaims when she sees the blood blossoming through my gown, "Now what happened here?"

"Sorry, ma'am, didn't mean to rip them like that," I reply, accepting that it was indeed my fault.

After the nurse calls in the doctor, he redoes my sutures. Once finished, he gives me the all clear to be discharged, so now I have to anxiously await the paperwork.

Once I get through all the formalities, the three of us make our way to Franklin's jeep. Since we were kids, he has always wanted one, so I surprised him with one two years ago for his birthday; it's all he drives now.

Given the somberness in the air, the drive is mostly quiet while we all try to connect invisible dots.

Mel, *my sweet, sweet Mel.* Her screams are still bouncing around in my head like the sweetest lullaby. I've had her for four days now, but I have yet to reveal my face. It's not the right time.

The first day I kept her locked in a dark room, letting the fear sink into her bones.

The second day I took her out for a little show. She didn't appreciate the pearl necklace I gave her on her neck and chest, but that's ok. She sang for me all the same when I got out the knife and had a little fun.

The third day I made her worship my cock on her knees. I held a knife to her pretty neck, but when that didn't work, I stabbed the knife through her hand. When she screamed I stuffed my cock so far into her throat that she choked. I fucked her face all while the tears streamed down her face. I took those tears and rubbed them on my cock, letting her see me use all of her as I see fit.

It's day four and I'm just beginning to think of all the fun I could have with my sweet song.

Twenty-Five
Melody

I'm shaking from the cold concrete floor that I'm chained to. The room is pitch black, without any windows for light to seep in through. Yesterday, he cut off all my clothes so I have nothing to ward off the cold.

My entire body is hurting from all the cuts he's inflicted on me, but the one that hurts the most is my hand. I want to gag when I think about what he made me do, how repulsed I now feel about myself.

I'm terrified when I think about what he could possibly do to me today. Sometimes he uses my body, and other times he just wants to hurt me. He slices my body open so he can watch me bleed, like he's trying to make sure I'm real and alive. I've lost count of the days I've been held here. It's hard to keep track when you're kept in a windowless room with no concept of time.

I've begun to lose hope that I'll even make it out of here alive. He tells me that Jaxon's car went up in flames when he took me from the scene of the accident and how his screams were the last thing he heard as he drove away. He thoroughly extinguished all hope that I had of Jax finding me. I feel the tears run down my cheeks. I did this to Jax; he didn't deserve the death he got. It's all my fault. I should have stayed far away from him the moment the pearls were left in my closet. At least that way, the only person that would have gotten hurt is myself.

I start to hear footsteps down the hall and instantly my body goes taut. I huddle into myself, trying to hide as much of my body that I can. He's coming for me. I start shaking in absolute terror... What will he do to me today?

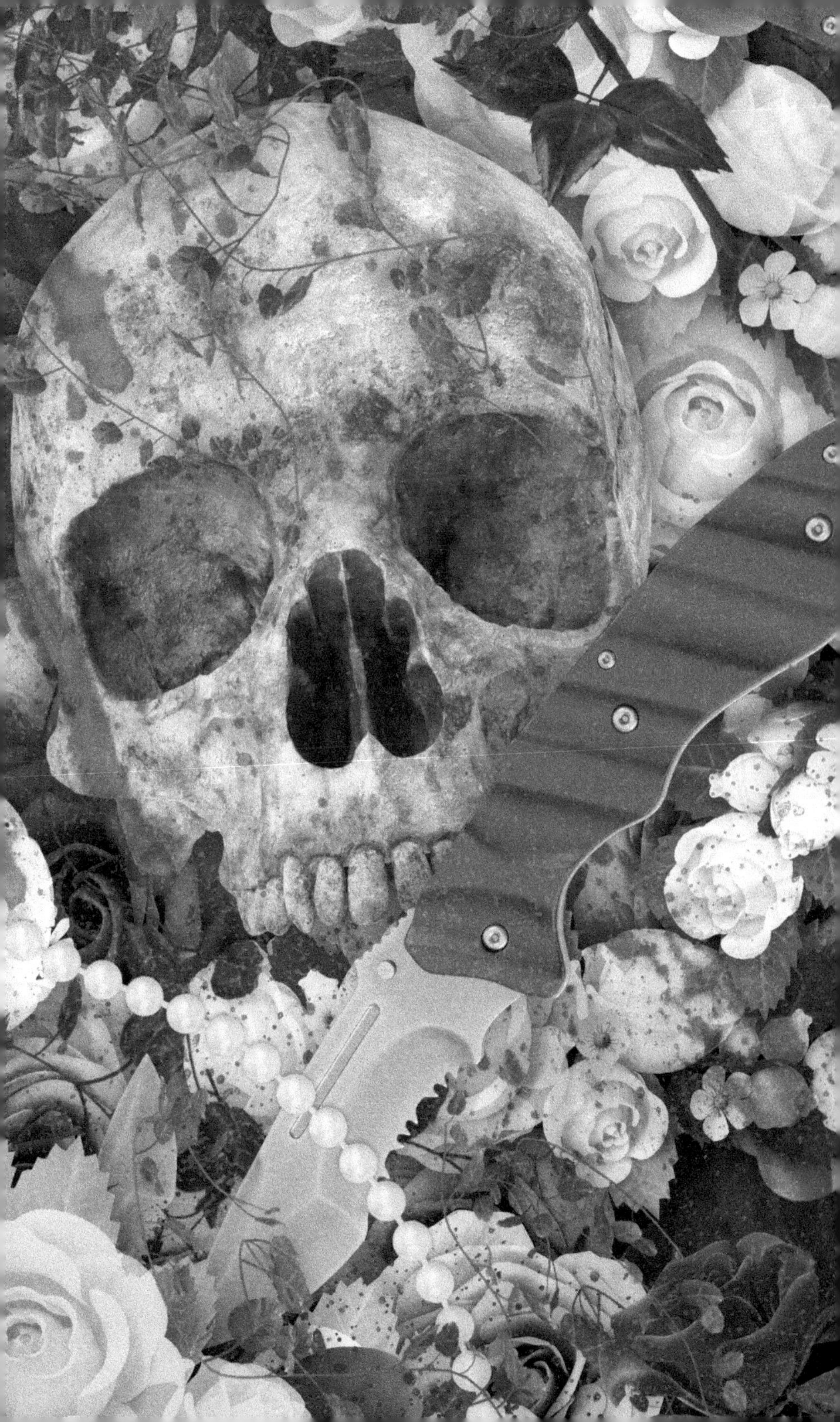

08:45

Twenty-Six

Jaxon

Once we pull up to Franklin's house, we all get out and make our way inside. Franklin pours each of us a glass of scotch, and we get to work.

I know there is some sort of link between her school and her attacker, I just don't know what it is. Or maybe there's not, and I'm overlooking something so obvious because I'm too focused on it. I'm beyond frustrated. Not having Melody in my arms is an agony I wouldn't wish on anyone. I miss her so much.

Franklin gives each of us the same documents so we can all review them in case anything was missed.

"Franklin, did you ever look into her graduating class to see if there was any connection when Jaxon asked you before," James asks.

"I did, yeah. I couldn't find any correlation between her and the attacker," Franklin replies, looking up from the file he holds.

The three of us grow more and more frustrated as the night wears on. I hate to even think what Melody is being put through. I refuse to even think that he's killed her. He wouldn't go through all this trouble just to get rid of her right away. No, he's about as obsessed with her as I am, but he definitely has me beat on the psycho scale.

We've all agreed we won't be going to the cops if we discover who this is and where he's holding her. James has connections to the Bonetti family who runs the Italian mafia along the west coast. He'll be calling in some favors for how we plan on handling this guy. I can't wait to get my hands on him. He's going to wish he was never born by the time we are done with him.

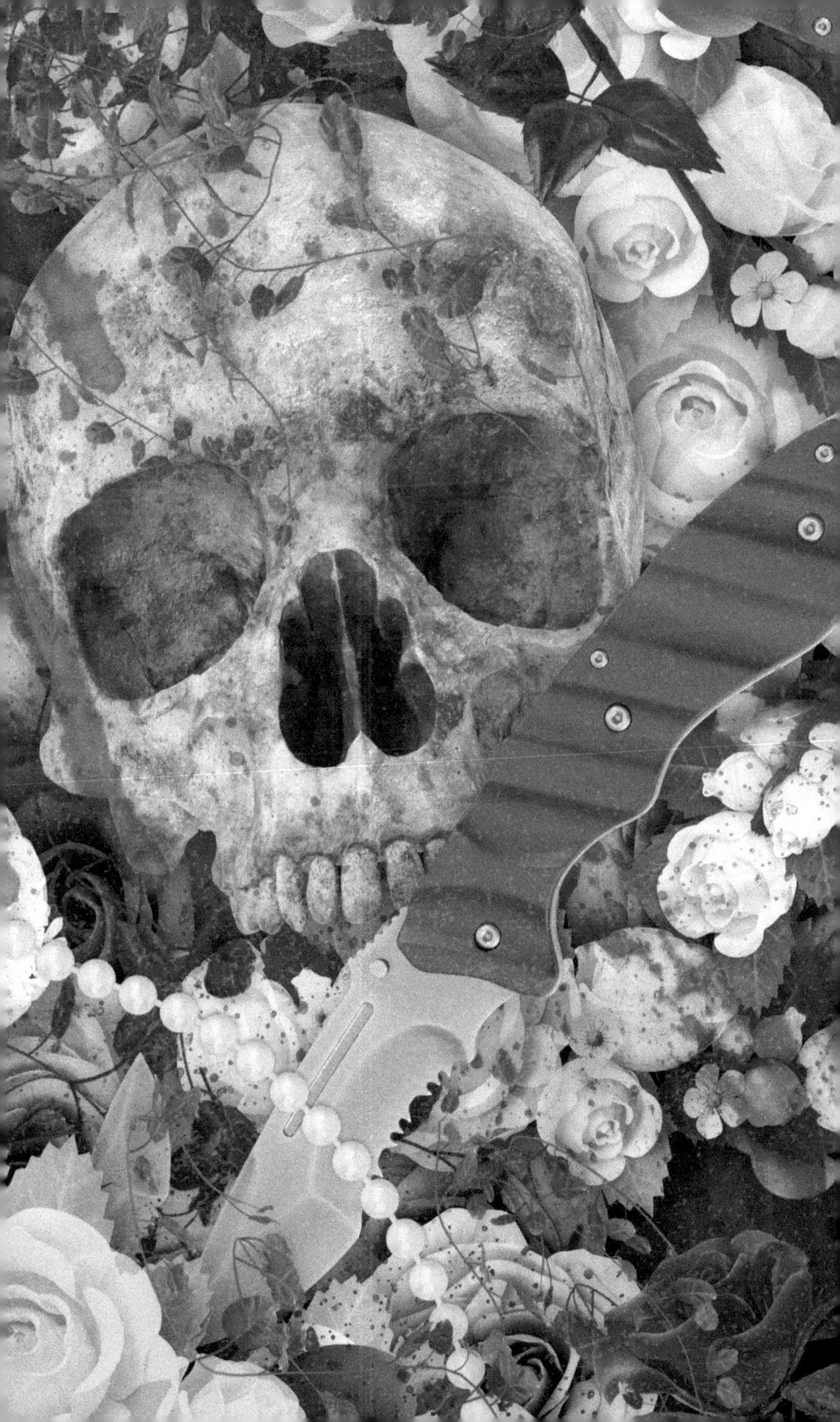

Twenty-Seven
Melody

I just want to die and be done with all of this. A part of me wishes each time he comes for me that he will just end me instead of continuing to inflict these monstrosities on me. I have nothing more to give. I've been used and abused, and there is no light at the end of the tunnel.

I shiver sitting in this dark room. I haven't eaten or drank anything since I was brought here. I feel so weak. I know I can only go so long without any water. I have become numb to the hunger pangs, however, my thirst for water is all consuming.

He came for me earlier today. He made me dance while he jerked himself off. If I didn't dance or I stopped, I was whipped. I have so many lashes on my back that I lost count. At first, I tried not to scream, tried not to give him the satisfaction, but it only lasted a few minutes. By the time the skin on my back split, I was screaming in pain with every slash of the whip. I danced as my blood dripped down my legs and splattered the concrete floor.

Afterwards, he put some sort of salve on my back and secured me in my chains back in the dark room. The fact that he even attended to my wounds tells me he plans on keeping me around for a while. At this point, I just pray that I will eventually die of dehydration. Death would be so much kinder than this hell I'm being forced to endure.

It's been hours since then and my back is on fire. I can't move without experiencing agonizing pain. While I try to move into a more comfortable position, which is near impossible, I hear his footsteps returning.

The key slides into the lock and I hear the door open. I close my eyes against the brightness as he turns on the overhead lights. My entire body is trembling with fear. When I don't hear any movement, I slowly lift my head and open my eyes to a mere squint. He has his mask on like usual, but this time instead of a knife or a whip, he's holding a glass of water.

"Would you like some water, my sweet Melody," he asks, his voice altered by some sort of device. Although I don't want to give him the satisfaction of saying yes, I nod my head. I hate to think what he would do to me if I disappointed him by saying no.

He walks over and holds out the glass of water. Just as I'm about to grab it, he pulls it out of my reach. "*Tsk, tsk, tsk.* Where are your manners, Melody? You didn't say please."

My eyes widen in fear as I hurriedly get out a "please" to placate him. Satisfied, he hands me the water and I greedily start gulping it down, water spilling down my chin and onto my chest. Once I'm done, I hold the glass back out to him, averting my eyes to the ground.

Faster than I can blink he's slapping the glass out of my hand, and it shatters in front of me. He grabs a fistful of my hair and pulls me to a standing position. My teeth clench with the pain, and I feel the wounds on my back stretching open again. Tears are spilling down my face.

"What did I say about manners, Melody? You can't even say *thank you*," he roars in my face.

"I-I-I'm s-sorry," I stutter out a reply through my tears. His grasp on my hair feels like he's ripping out all of my hair from my head. "Th-thank you."

"It's a little too late for that now, Melody. I'm going to have to teach you the manners you so desperately need."

Terrified for what he has in store, I try to fight out of his grasp, my body going into survival mode. I manage to escape his hands, but there's nowhere for me to go; I'm still chained to the floor.

Trying to get as far away from him as possible, I back myself into the corner of the room, adrenaline rushing through my body.

He stalks towards me and grabs me by the arm. "Fuck you, Melody. You should be grateful for everything I do for you. I tend to your wounds and bring you water, and this is the treatment I get?" He is certifiably insane... He thinks he's doing me favors? I wouldn't have all these wounds on my body if it weren't for him. I know something is coming but I have no idea what.

Before I can even blink, he grabs me by the throat and slams me against the wall. I have flashbacks to the night of my attack, and I fight with desperation. He fumbles with his belt and I attempt to hit and kick him wherever I can. Anything to stop what I know is coming.

In my feeble attempt to fight him off, my nails bite into his skin, and I'm struggling to hold him off. His grip tightens on my neck and my vision starts to darken around the edges. No, no, not this again. Please god, no. I'm sobbing but desperately trying to fight him off. It won't be enough though. It wasn't enough the first time, and it won't be enough now. He undoes his belt and the zipper of his jeans. Grabbing his dick he attempts to line up with my entrance, but I'm twisting and turning, hoping to god I can avoid him. In one last desperate attempt to get him to stop, I rip his mask right off his face.

He's staring at me in shock at first, but his face slowly distorts into anger.

"You stupid little bitch..." He punches me in the face and I hear the snap in my nose, followed by blood trickling into my mouth. My head snaps back and hits the concrete wall. I'm seeing stars as my body slumps to the ground.

"Surprised to see me, Melody?"

All I can do is look up at him with disgust in my eyes. I would have never expected it to be him. I wouldn't have even imagined he was capable of doing the things he's done to me.

The shock is finally catching up with my body, all of the energy completely drained from my very soul.

Once again, my vision darkens until there is nothing more.

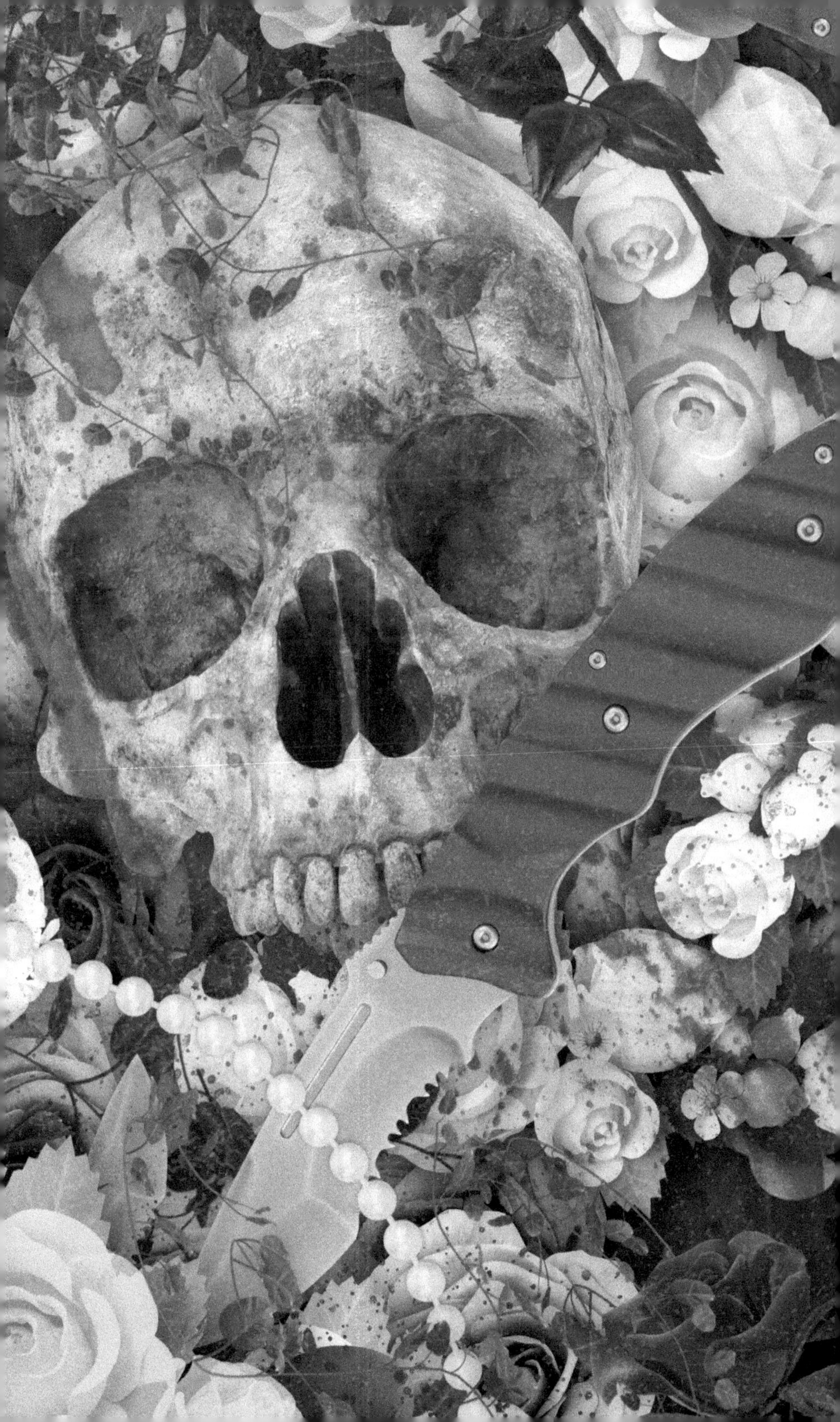

08:45

TWENTY-EIGHT

JAXON

It's three in the morning and we're all still awake. Refusing to give up, we read through everything we have for the tenth time. James called Kayden earlier, so now he's here as well, looking over everything on Franklin's laptop.

"We should probably get some rest," says Franklin, yawning and stretching his arms.

"We won't be any help to Melody if we don't rest and go at this again in a few hours with fresh minds."

I slam my file down on the table. "Melody might not have a few more hours, Franklin. We have to keep looking."

James puts a hand on my shoulder. "Franklin is right, Jax. We have to be at our very best, and we can't do that if we're running on no sleep."

Shrugging his hand off my shoulder, I tell them to go ahead without me. There is no way I am sleeping without Melody at my side.

Kayden is the only one that stays behind with me. I don't know why that is, maybe because he's used to club hours and staying up 'til 6 A.M. Whatever the reason, I'm grateful for it. Kayden has always been more of a loner and rarely comes to our family dinners or spends time with any of us on holidays.

However, I feel like he knows how important Melody is to me, and I'm really just grateful for any help we can get right now.

Kayden sets down his file and moves back over to Franklin's laptop to watch the video recording of the masked attacker. His distorted voice comes through the speakers and I turn back to my file, combing through everything for the twentieth time. I'm so desperate, I feel tears building in my eyes. I'm exhausted and still hurting from the car accident, but I can't stop. I need Melody back in my arms, safe and sound where she belongs.

"Where is 305?"

"What?"

Kayden turns to me fully. "I said, where is 305? He mentions in the video, '*I smell you all around me, much like in 305.*' What is that supposed to mean?"

"I don't know, play it again."

I don't understand how we missed this... but *what does it mean?*

I rush up the stairs to Franklin's second floor and burst into his room.

"Wha—" Before Franklin can even get a word out, I'm turning on the light and telling him to get up. James comes in a second later, looking between the two of us.

"I think Kayden found something."

After bringing my brother and Franklin downstairs, Kayden played the clip over again for them.

"Do any of you know what 305 pertains to?"

They both shake their head no, and it feels like we take two steps forward and one step back. This might be something or it might be nothing at all. In my gut though, I have a feeling that the guy messed up. He said himself that Melody makes him uncontrollable. This is something big, and I'm going to figure this out.

Each of us are turning back to our files; we scan them for any mention of 305.

What feels like hours later, I finally come across a 305.

"I got something," I announce to the group. My heart is racing, and I truly believe this will lead us to Melody. My little sparrow has to be so afraid, and the thought alone kills me.

"OK, so what is it?" asks Franklin as he takes a seat next to me.

"I was looking over her school records and stumbled upon a course number that ends in 305. It's one of the advanced classes she was taking, so it probably won't be with anyone from her graduating class."

"Holy shit... OK let me go to my laptop and see if I can pull up info on who was in that class with her."

A few minutes later, Franklin turns in his chair and has a smirk on his face. Why he always leaves us hanging is beyond me.

"What did you find Franklin? Spill it," says Kayden, looking like he wants to throttle his neck.

"There were forty-three students in that course and twenty-six of them were males. Not sure how else to narrow it down, I sorted through Melody's course work and found a few projects that she worked on with guys in the classroom. One of them stood out to me though. His name is Damian Merikh, and he did quite a lot of projects and essays with her. When I did a search on him, I found that he owns multiple properties in Southern California, but what I found really interesting is that he owns a few warehouses in downtown Silicon Valley."

"Holy shit, if this is the guy, how do we narrow down which warehouse Melody might be in?" I ask, getting up from my seat and starting to pace the room. My little sparrow is coming home, I feel it in my bones.

"Well, that's the thing. So I checked the surrounding area for cameras. Only one of the properties has cameras across the street, and I could see the entrance to the warehouse in the camera footage. Going back through video footage for the past week, the first warehouse has absolutely no movement. So that eliminates that building—at least I hope."

Franklin continues, "So now we are down to two buildings. One is newer and has a legit business running out of it, so I doubt he would keep her where there are people coming in and out. That leaves the last building. According to google images, it's pretty run down, but there aren't very many windows and the windows it does have, appear completely blacked out. I think this is the one."

"Let's go then," Kayden says gruffly, running a hand through his hair. "We can't really afford to waste any time."

"We need to think about this, make a plan. We can't just go in all willy-nilly," says James, being his typical rational self.

"What do we do?" I ask, feeling hope simmering in my chest for the first time in four days.

We all put our heads together for an hour or two and come up with a solid plan.

We're going to bring Melody home if it's the last thing we do.

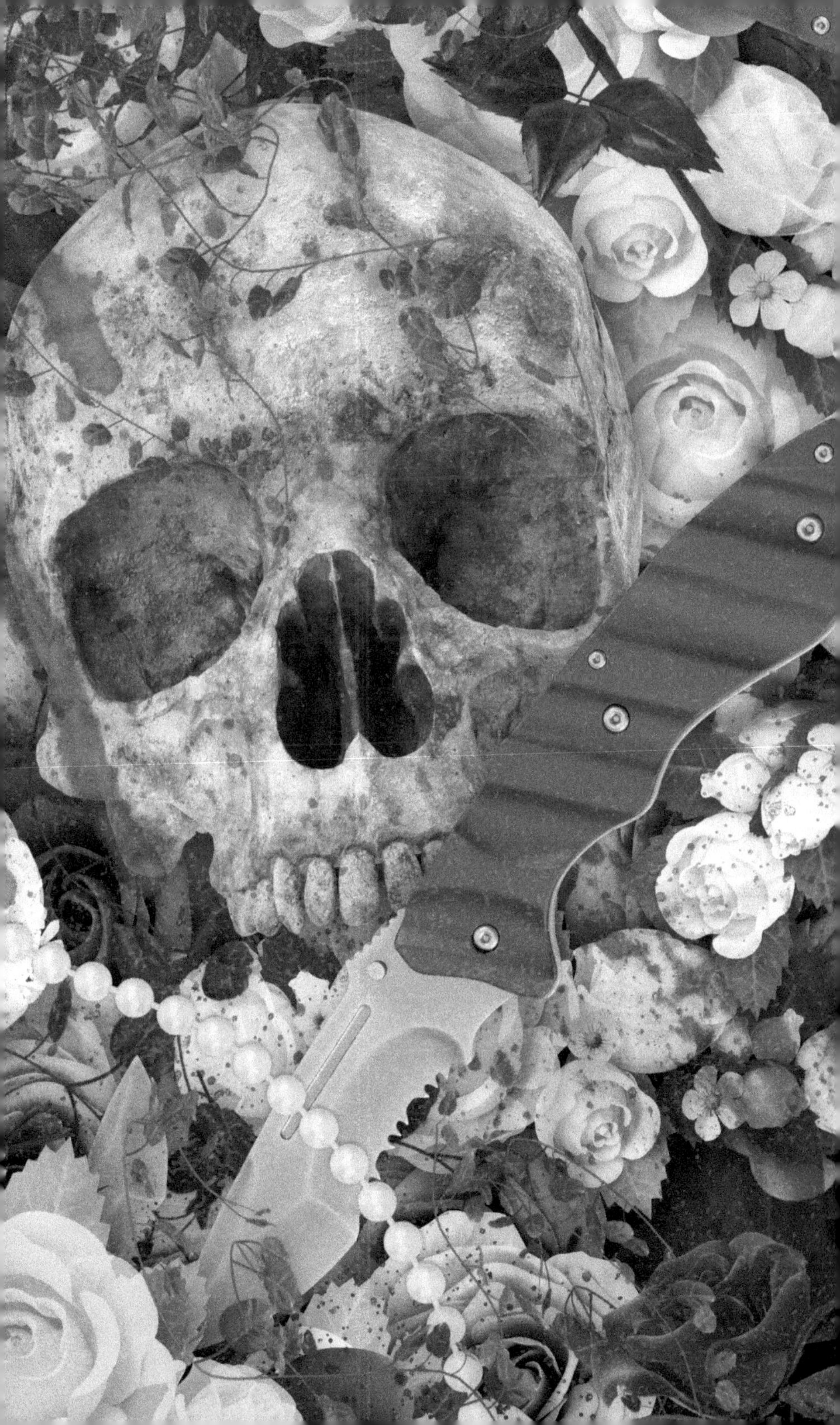

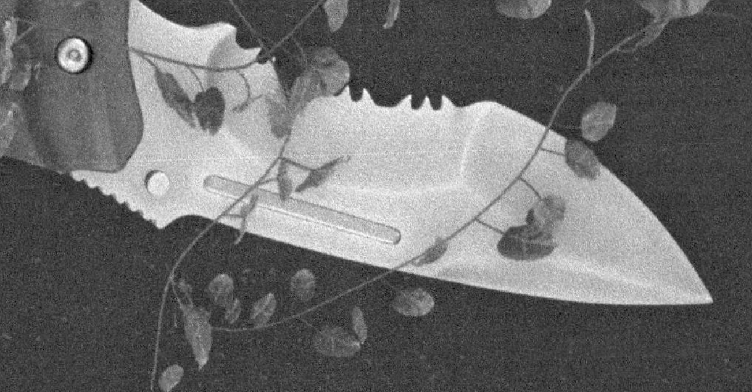

CHAPTER 28.5

DAMIAN

The stupid little bitch tore my mask off right as I was about to take that tight cunt of hers.

Completely overcome with rage, I kick her in the ribs where she lays on the concrete floor. She's completely passed out, but I still get enjoyment from kicking her even though I don't have her beautiful screams to fill the silence. I grab a fistful of her hair and lift her head up off the floor. Completely passed out. *Pfft*, useless.

I could see the recognition in her eyes before she passed out though. Our time in school together is something she probably overlooked. We did all our homework together in the school library after classes, stayed up late talking about anything and everything. I was the only one that realized Brian didn't deserve her, that he would never be enough for her. We had been close at one point. So *easily* she forgot about me though... The thought just pisses me off even more. I'll show that bitch, she'll never be able to forget me when I'm done with her.

Taking my cock out of my pants, I stroke myself a few times before crouching down over Melody's prone form, grabbing a handful of her tit. Massaging her breast and flicking her now hardened nipple with one hand, I grab her other hand with my own and put it on my cock. Taking her hand in mine, I continue stroking myself. The softness of her skin against my raging erection sends shivers down my spine. I wish it was her mouth around my cock, but I'll take whatever I can get.

Increasing the pace, I pinch her nipple and slowly start to see her come to. She cracks her eyes open and seeing what I'm doing, tries to yank her hand away. I keep a tight grip on her hand and continue making her pump me.

"Take your other hand, Melody, and massage my balls," I demand of her.

Knowing what the repercussions of not obeying me are, she promptly reaches out and cups my balls, massaging them between her fingers.

"You like that, Mel? You like jerking me off, don't you?"

She looks down and nods her head; her words must be escaping her. Taking my hand off her breast, I move down her stomach and grab her pussy. I violently shove two fingers into her tight cunt, making her yelp in pain. It's a symphony to my ears and it only turns me on even more.

"I'm going to remove my hand, Mel. You are going to keep stroking me, is that understood? You know what will happen if you stop? I'll stuff my cock into that tight cunt of yours instead of my fingers."

She obeys beautifully. Kneeling down, I reposition myself so that I can finger fuck her and play with her tits at the same time. She's so magnificent, tears streaming down her face, her lower lip trembling in fear. It's fucking beautiful. None of the other women I took could ever compare to her. The more she strokes me, the more her hand starts to split open again from when I stabbed her. Her blood is mixing wonderfully with my precum, painting my cock in a beautiful shade of red.

Feeling myself coming to the edge, I instruct Melody to let go of me and lay back down. Standing up, I move over her and continue to stroke myself at a grueling pace. I come with a roar and spill my cum all over her hot body, coating her breasts and stomach. It's the most beautiful piece of art I've ever made.

Thinking this masterpiece needs one more item to make it perfect, I pull out Melody's pearl necklace and clasp it around her neck. There, she's beautiful.

"Tonight, Melody, you'll once again be mine. I'm going to take that tight cunt of yours, and you're going to enjoy every minute of it. By the end of the night, you'll be screaming my name to the heavens."

Twenty-Nine

My hand is stinging. He made me jerk him off with the hand he put a knife through, and now I'm bleeding everywhere again. I am hopeless. After he finished he donned the pearls around my throat, and then he threw a towel from his back pocket at me to clean myself up with. Usually he just lets me sit with his mess all over me. I clean off as fast as I can, throwing the towel across the room.

When he left he turned off the lights again, so I'm now plunged back into darkness. I feel around for the chain secured to my ankle and try again to pull it from the floor. It's useless though, I don't have the strength to do anything but cause myself more pain. I give up and huddle back into the corner of the room.

I can't believe I didn't think of him sooner, but then again why would I have? In school, he seemed like a normal person. He never came off like he liked me or that he was obsessive over me. Nothing to set off any alarms at least. We would work on our homework a lot together which meant staying at the library pretty late sometimes, but I never got the feeling or notion that he liked me more than just friends.

I'm terrified of what's to come later tonight. I've been lucky so far that he hasn't attempted to rape me, but it sounds like my luck has finally run out. Tears run down my cheeks, but instead of feeling fear and anger, all I feel is resignation. I think I have come to accept that no one is going to save me, not the police and certainly not Jax. Thinking his name causes my heart to stutter. I was falling for him so hard only for him to be ripped from me before we really had a chance to explore our relationship further.

And what kills me is that the last thing we said to each other was a stupid argument about money for the repairs to my house. It seems so ridiculous now.

I wish I had kissed him one last time, if only to help me get through what is coming.

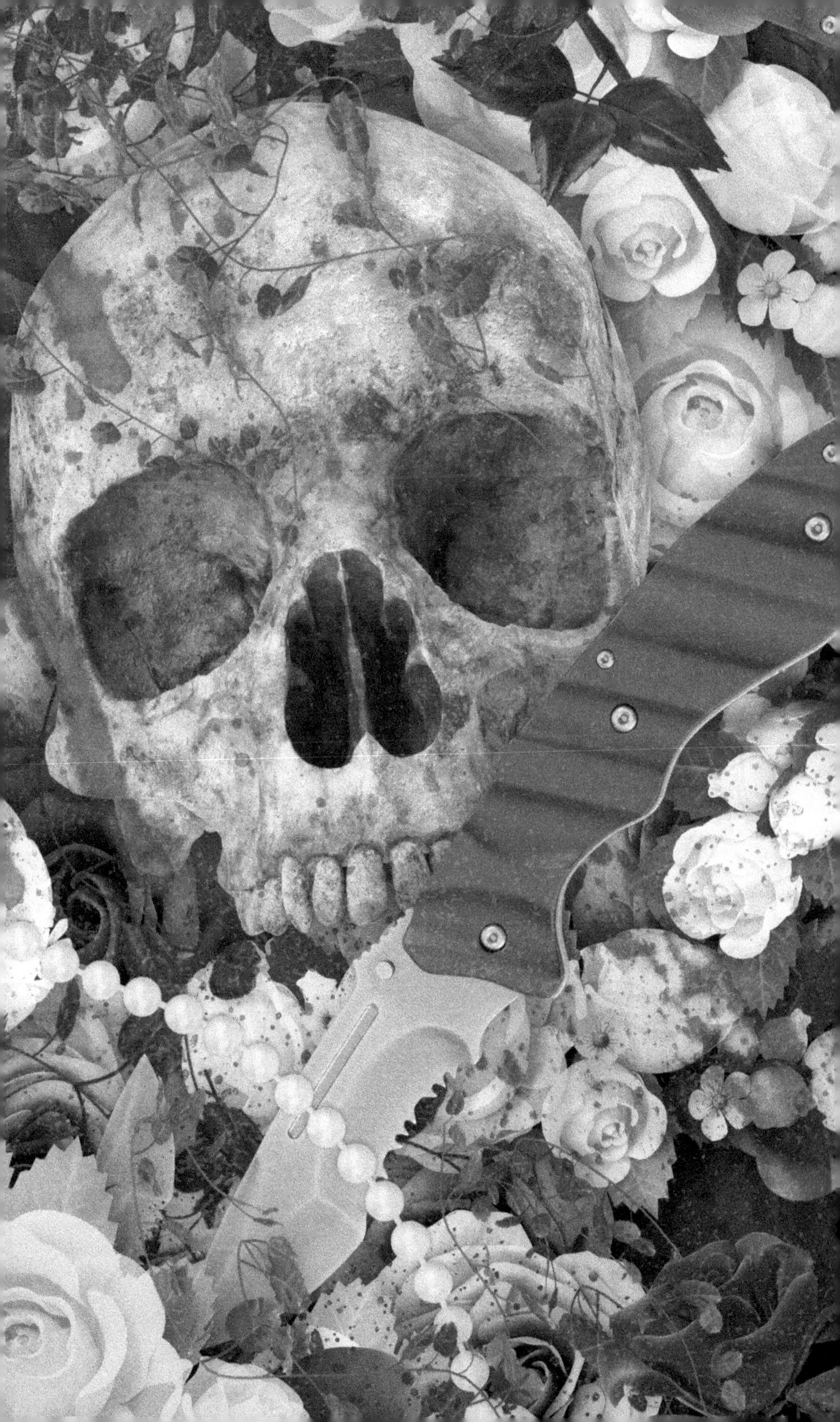

THIRTY

JAXON

Prepping ourselves with guns and knives from Franklin's safe, we gather whatever we can from his limited arsenal. With most of the items hidden on our person, we get ready to bring Melody back home. Taking Franklin's jeep, we head to Silicon Valley. The drive takes us an hour and a half, but we finally make it.

Cutting the lights to Franklin's jeep, we crawl to a stop to avoid attention. There we see a guy leaving the warehouse that matches the photo that Franklin pulled up of Damian.

After he locks up, he heads to his vehicle and takes off. Wasting no time, we put in our earpieces so that we can all communicate with each other and Franklin. James, Kayden, and I make our way to the building walking nonchalantly. Franklin stays in the vehicle to be our lookout.

Breaking the lock on the door, Kayden pushes it open and waves for us to follow him inside. Not seeing any type of security system, we shut the door and move further into the dark building. The building was definitely a warehouse of some sort at one time, and it's absolutely massive. Sticking to the plan, and equipped with our flashlights, James goes to the right, Kayden to the left, and I head straight down the hall.

Opening a door on the left with my gun and flashlight raised, I find nothing but empty boxes so I keep moving. On the far end of the hall is a set of double doors. As I make my way over to them, I quickly check all the rooms as I go. Opening the double doors, I'm brought into a large open space where all the manufacturing must have occurred at one point. In the middle of the room is a drain, and from where I'm standing I see a puddle surrounding the hole.

I make my way closer, dread turning my stomach. As I shine my flashlight over the puddle, it glows crimson, and I almost lose the contents of my stomach. What did he do to her? Turning in a slow circle, I look around to see if there are any other rooms I missed. My eyes catch on a door behind some machinery. I make my way over and just as I'm about to open the door, I'm met with resistance. Locked.

Pushing the button on my earpiece, I tell the guys to come to the center of the warehouse and that I found a locked door. All I get is radio silence from Franklin, strange. Setting down my gun and flashlight, I try to pick the lock to no avail. I was never skilled at picking locks, that is most definitely Kayden's area of expertise.

"If you knew what was good for you, you'd step away from that fuckin' door."

I freeze. Slowly turning my body, I'm met with Damian standing behind my brothers. Holding a gun in each hand, he prods my brothers along until they stop just in front of me.

I give my brothers a look and turn my attention to him. "So... how is this going to play out Damian?"

"I'll tell you how it's going to play out, Jaxon Stonewell. Yes, don't look too shocked. You and I are aren't all that different. I've seen you hunting my Mel since that first day at the bookstore. However, once I saw you with Melody at her house the night I trashed the place, I made certain to do some research on you."

"But that's not important right now. You're going to step away from that fucking door and if you don't, I'll shoot one of your brothers here through their fucking head."

Following his orders, I step away from the door with my hands raised up in surrender.

"Good, now get on your knees, motherfucker."

I slowly sink to my knees, never breaking eye contact with my brothers in the hopes that one of them is quicker with their blade than he is with his gun.

"You're a fuckin' pain in my ass. If it weren't for you, I would have had my sweet Melody so much sooner. I would have been able to sink my cock in that tight cunt of hers repeatedly by now. You took her from me and for that, you're going to pay." He moves the gun from behind Kayden and brings it to my forehead. Waiting for one of my brothers to make their move, I close my eyes as he cocks the gun.

The gunshot rings out close to my head, and my ears start to ring. Opening my eyes, I take in the scene before me. Kayden has a knife buried in Damian's side, and James has secured both guns from his grasp. How they moved so fast is beyond me, but I'm just grateful I'm still alive.

"Search him for a key," I tell Kayden. Searching him, Kayden finally finds a set of keys in his front pocket and hands them to me.

"Go get Melody, Jax. We have it covered."

Turning back toward the door, I hear James and Kayden laying punches into the guy. I'll let them have their fun before I get my turn. Part of me is wondering what happened to Franklin and why he didn't alert us, but right now Melody is my top concern.

Trying each key, I start to get frustrated that none of them are working. Finally, I get to the last key and hope blossoms in my chest as the lock turns.

Opening the door, all I see is darkness. Unsure where the light switch is, I squint my eyes and just barely make out someone huddled deep in a corner in the room. Trepidation fills me as I wonder if it's Melody and if she's alive. Reaching a hand out along the wall, I finally find the light switch and flip it on.

The sight before me has me shocked to my very core. My little sparrow huddles in a corner, face buried in her knees. Her body is riddled with bruises and slashes. Her back is split open in various spots as though she was whipped within an inch of her life. My jaw clenches and I shake with barely controlled rage. As I step further in the room, I see Melody start to tense up and huddle even further into herself.

"Little sparrow..." I say, coaxing her to look at me. I walk slowly towards her, not wanting to startle her.

"Little sparrow, look at me."

She turns her head to the side and her eyes widen. She drops her arms from around her knees. "Jaxon? But how?"

"Shhh, I'm here now, baby."

"But he said you died, he said he heard your screams... You burned to death..."

"He lied, little sparrow, I'm right here." I crouch down and reach out a hand to comfort her, but my hand just hovers. I'm unsure where to touch her without causing her more pain.

Her voice catches on a sob and next thing I know she's throwing her arms around me. I'm careful not to touch her back so I simply hold her head to me. She lets everything out and all I can do is hold her as she cries and shakes with all her pent up adrenaline.

Pulling her arms from around me, I grab her face as gently as I possibly can.

"My little sparrow, you're safe now. I've got you." I kiss her forehead tenderly and grab her hand to pull her up. She hisses through her teeth in pain, and I immediately let go of her hand. Looking down, I turn her hand in mine and finally see the stab wound. That motherfucker.

"Fuck, baby, I'm sorry. I didn't see it."

"It's ok, Jax. I know you didn't mean to."

Taking off my button down shirt, I hand it over to her so she can put it on. As she does, I notice the pearl necklace around her neck. "Melody, do you want that necklace on you?"

When she shakes her head no, I move behind her to take it off and then throw them on the ground.

Next, I take off my jeans and briefs, handing her the briefs so she can put them on. Once I help her into the briefs, I put my jeans back on and I lead her from the room.

The scene before me fills me with renewed rage, and I'm ready to kill.

Thirty-One

Melody

I see, as well as feel, Jaxon trembling with rage. James and Kayden are holding Damian up with each arm behind his back. He smiles up at me with blood coating his teeth. Blood drips from his hands; looks like the brothers had some fun cutting off a few fingers.

"Hello, my sweet Melody. Miss me already?"

"Don't you dare talk to her," Jaxon growls before landing a punch in Damian's gut. He doubles over but not before the brothers are lifting him back up.

They hold him as Jax lays into him, punching every possible part of his upper body. When Damian slumps forward again Jax grabs his hair and forces him to look up at him.

"Thought you'd get off that easy, huh? You think this is all we got... We are just getting started you piece of shit!"

I flinch with every hit that lands on him, not because I sympathize with him, but because I've grown accustomed to being hit myself over these last few days. The sound brings back all the memories, and I grab Jax's arm just before he lays into him again. I've noticed blood starting to seep through his shirt, too.

"Jax, enough. I want to go home. I hurt all over..."

"Fuck, I'm sorry, baby. You know we aren't going to turn him in right? We aren't letting him leave here alive..."

"I know, Jax, that's why I have one request before we leave..." I pull Jax away from the others.

"Anything, little sparrow. Tell me what you want."

"I want you to cut off his dick and shove it down *his* throat... See how he likes it."

My last statement causes Jaxon's jaw to tick; he's barely holding himself together from just outright killing this guy at my admission. I said without so many words exactly what I was subjected to in this hell hole, and I know Jaxon picks up on it.

"You got it, baby, but are you sure you want to watch this?"

"Abso-fucking-lutely."

Without wasting any more time, James and Kayden start pulling down Damian's pants all the while he is fighting with renewed energy. Jax grabs him by the throat and brings his face close to his. I can't make out what was said, but Damian's eyes widen in fear.

They stuff the towel from the room where I was kept into his mouth and drop his boxers around his thighs. James gives Jaxon a pair of leather gloves that he must have had in his pocket, and before I can even blink an eye, Jaxon uses Damian's own knife to cut his dick off. He removes the towel and Damian is shrieking as blood spurts from his body, puddling beneath him as he squirms. Jaxon uses the opportunity to shove it down his throat.

We all watch as he thrashes his head back and forth trying to be rid of himself. His entire body convulses with pain, and his face turns purple as he chokes on his own dick. Satisfied that he got exactly what was coming to him, I tell Jax to end it so we can finally go home.

James grabs the gun from his waistband as Kayden steps back and lets go of Damian. Without anyone holding him up, he falls to the ground, cracking his teeth on the concrete. Quicker than I can even process, James shoots him in the head. Blood and brain matter pools beneath him, and I let out the breath I was holding. I'm finally free of him.

"Jax, please, can we go now?"

"Absolutely, little sparrow."

"I'll call in that favor and have this cleaned up and taken care of," says James reassuringly.

"Thanks, man, I appreciate it," Jax replies, clapping a hand on James's shoulder.

"Kayden, you stayin' or goin'?"

"I'll stay here and help James, go on without me."

We say our goodbyes and Jax and I head outside. Parked across the street is a jeep and what appears to be Franklin slumped forward in the seat.

Cursing under his breath, Jax runs up to the driver's side, opens the door, and places a hand on his neck.

"Thank god, he has a pulse. Must be knocked out or something."

After Jaxon gets Franklin in the backseat, he comes around and gets me settled in the passenger seat.

Now that I'm finally safe, the adrenaline that has been coursing through my veins dissipates, leaving me exhausted and shaky. As Jaxon drives us home, I steal glances at him every so often. I can't believe he's alive and real. I spent the last five days believing him to be dead, and here he is, my avenging god.

As the landscape fades from the city lights to the green and blue coastline, I start to drift asleep, the exhaustion *finally* catching up with me.

08:45

Thirty-Two

Jaxon

After getting Franklin awake, I drop him off at his house with his jeep. I shoot off a text to Brooke so that she can come keep an eye on him for the night.

Ever so carefully transferring Melody to my BMW, we make our way to my house.

After getting Melody up into my suite and settled onto my bed, I go in the bathroom and start the bathtub. Knowing that she has so many injuries, I want to get her cleaned up before the doctor comes over and treats her wounds. Making sure the water isn't too hot, but also not too cold, I turn off the spout and make my way back to the room to grab Melody.

"Little sparrow, wake up... I need you to wake up for me, gorgeous."

Melody flinches at my touch and my heart breaks all over again. I tell myself I can't fix what happened, but I can damn well try to mend her.

"Lift your arms for me, baby," I tell her as she finally sits up.

I take off her shirt and throw it aside, trying my best to ignore all the blood that has soaked through the shirt from her back. If I allow myself to sit in my anger too long, I'll lose it.

Helping Melody stand up, I pull down the briefs and have her step out of them. Leading her to the bathroom, I help to gently lower her in the tub. She gasps as she lowers into the water, her injuries probably stinging and incredibly painful. Knowing that her injuries are very sensitive right now, I grab a soft washcloth for her to wash herself with. I hold up her hair as she washes the back of her neck, laying a tender kiss to the top of her head.

"Jaxon, I'm so sorry, there wasn't anyth—"

I cut her off before she can say anything more. "What in the world are you apologizing for, little sparrow?"

"Everything he did to me... I couldn't stop it."

"Melody, stop. I am in no way upset with you. At all. I can only imagine the horrors you were put through... You are so incredibly strong for surviving. And I'm damn happy you did, you hear me? I wouldn't have been able to live without you. You are such an integral part of me, I can't function without you next to me."

Melody looks up at me through her lashes. "Are you sure, Jax? I'm dirty..."

I grab her chin and make her look at me. "Melody Ann Harper, you *WILL NOT* say such things about yourself, am I understood? You are beautiful and the strongest woman I know. You will not give that fucker's ghost the satisfaction of keeping you down. You will overcome this and I'll be right by your side every step of the way. I don't care how long it takes, you have me, all of me, through the entire journey and the rest of our lives. Do you understand?"

She peers into my eyes, looking for a lie. "OK, Jax, I understand... I believe you."

"Good, now that that's settled, let's get you out of this tub before you catch a cold."

"I'm sure that's the reason..." she has the audacity to smirk at me. My little sparrow, cut and bloodied up all over her body, and who knows what other horrors she had to endure, is still the sassy vixen I've come to know and love.

Wrapping her in a towel, I kiss her nose. "I love you, Melody, with every part of my soul, I love you. Like the sky filled with stars, you light me up. You are my northern star and I, a wayward shepherd. I'll follow you to the ends of the earth, because you are my true home."

Thirty-Three

Melody

After helping me towel off and get into a pair of underwear, Jaxon instructs me to lay on my stomach on the bed. He explained that the doctor will be here shortly, and the first thing he's going to look at is my back and my hand.

As we wait, I ask Jaxon the question I've been burning to ask since he found me.

"How did you find me, Jax? How did you know about Damian, about his warehouse, about everything?"

"Melody, promise you won't get mad?"

I nod. "I promise."

"I've been watching you for some time. Franklin, while he is my best friend, is also the best hacker south of Silicon Valley. I had him hack into your security system so I could keep an eye on you."

At this point I stare at him in disbelief, but I keep my mouth shut, so he keeps going. "The night Damian trashed your house, he actually left a message on your camera. I won't quote it, but he made mention of being in 305 with you. We finally figured out that it was one of your courses, and then we narrowed it down even further to who you worked on projects with the most. We ran the names through Franklin's database, and Damian is the one that seemed most suspicious, owning numerous abandoned warehouses. That's how we found you."

My mouth hangs open, and I'm in complete disbelief about the lengths Jaxon went through to find me. I'm ready to argue with him about how crazy he sounds, but he cuts me off.

"Melody, please don't expect an apology from me about this. If I hadn't done what I did, we would have had no way, no clue, how to even find you. Saving you from that fucker is worth it."

I probably look like I'm still ready to argue, but I gather myself instead and say, "Thank you, Jax."

He's completely taken aback, probably because I just thanked him for stalking me. He feels my forehead to check for a fever, but I feel fine.

"I'm not delusional, Jax, I really am thankful that you guys found me. If that means I have to accept the fact that you stalked me, I'll accept it ten times over."

"But," I continue, "don't think you get to keep stalking me... We need healthy boundaries for this to work."

"Anything for you, little sparrow."

The doctor comes shortly after and takes a look at all of my injuries. The injuries on my back from being whipped needed stitches, sixty four in total. My hand was also stitched up. Luckily, the fucker missed my bones but did a pretty considerable amount of damage to the surrounding tissue and muscle. I have a few broken ribs which should heal on their own, and all the other cuts and bruises on my body will heal with time. He also set my broken nose, which hurt like hell.

Jaxon is given some ointments to use on my hand and my back to prevent infection and some pain pills to use while I'm healing. He also stitched Jaxon's stomach back up.

Walking to the door, Jaxon thanks the doctor for coming on such short notice and for going to see Franklin next. He hands him an extra stack of bills for providing services at such a late hour.

I'm about to protest and say I can pay for it, but the words die on my lips. I'm not going to start another argument over money. If he wants to pay for it, I'll let him.

Jaxon must spot the look on my face however, because he stalks over to me, one hand coming up to hold the back of my head and the other on my upper ass, gently pulling me to him.

"Melody, Melody, Melody... you weren't just about to protest me paying for the good doctor's services were you?"

"Never would I do such a thing." I smile up at him sweetly.

"Liar."

"I do have money though, Jax."

"Well until we have a shared bank account, we will be using *my* money," replies Jax, letting go of me to cross his arms over his chest.

I love when this man gets possessive and bossy; it's such a fucking turn on.

Batting my eyelashes at him, I sashay my way back into the bedroom. Or I try to sashay at least. It's a little hard to do with sixty four stitches in my back.

"Where do you think you're going, little sparrow?"

"I thought maybe you wanted to lay down and cuddle with me..."

"You bet your ass I do."

Jaxon follows me into the bedroom, and for once, things feel right in the world.

Thirty-Four

Jaxon

FOUR MONTHS LATER

Driving my new McLaren down into the garage, I park her near my lockers. Melody is waiting for me, all decked out in the riding gear I left on the bed for her this morning along with a handwritten note.

> *I left this riding gear for you. Let's go for a ride today ;)*
> *Meet me in the garage at 2pm.*

As I exit the car, Melody comes over and gives me a welcome home kiss, grabbing my ass and making me think of all the ways I can take her over the hood of my car. Before I can make good on any of my thoughts though, she drags me to my lockers and holds out my riding gear for me. Quickly changing into my gear and riding boots, I place my clothes and shoes on the bench.

Turning towards Melody, I take the new helmet I bought specifically for her and place it over her head, doing up her chin strap as well. Next, I put on my own helmet. Looking over at

Melody, I see she has her visor flipped up and her face has a smirk on it. Clueless as to what she's thinking, I pull her in and bump her helmet with mine.

"How was therapy, little sparrow?

"It was good, we talked about you a lot."

"Is that so?"

"Yep, not telling you anything though."

"Hmm, OK. Keep your secrets then... Are you excited to go for a ride, little sparrow?"

"Jax, about the ride..."

"What's wrong, Melody?"

"I think I may have a helmet kink, because seeing you in that helmet is making me so horny right now."

"Is that so?!"

She bites her lip, and it takes everything in me not to rip off her helmet and claim her lips right here and now. My booktok girl has a thing for a bikertok boy, it seems. Consider me claimed. *How did I get so lucky?*

Reaching up to take off my helmet, I'm stopped by Melody placing a hand over my own.

"Stop, Jax... I want you to keep it on."

Obliging my woman, I keep the helmet on and sit down on the bench. The moment Melody is within range, I grab her thighs and pull her into me, making her straddle my hips.

"How am I supposed to kiss you with my helmet on, little sparrow?"

"Hmm, you won't be doing any kissing, Jax," she says, lifting off my lap.

Letting her take control, she starts to take off her own helmet and riding gear, stripping down until she's left in her bra and a pair of cheeky panties. Walking towards me, she grips my gear and starts to unzip it. I stand up to allow her better access. She pulls down my gear until it's around my hips, allowing her to grab my cock and free it from the confines of my briefs.

"Is that what you were looking for, little sparrow?"

"Mmm," she replies, pushing me back down on the bench so my back is against the wall.

Lowering herself down onto her knees, she licks a scorching path from the base of my cock all the way to the tip, circling before taking me into her mouth where she sucks and teases all along my cock. Having her lips on me is heaven, and I swear I've died ten times over.

Popping off my cock, she looks up at me. Even though she can't see my face through the visor, she knows exactly what she's doing to me. "Do you like that, Jax? Do you like when I'm a little slut for you," she asks before taking my cock back into her mouth.

"Fuck yeah, baby." I grab a fistful of her hair and take over the rhythm. I'm thrusting into her mouth and she's taking me so well. I feel her gag and it takes all of me not to bust right then and there.

I lift her off my cock. "Bend over, little sparrow, let me see that ass."

Pushing her against the lockers, I push down between her shoulder blades until she's bent over at just the right angle. Moving her panties to the side, I find her already soaked. I swipe a finger through her wet folds and circle her clit before plunging two fingers into her tight pussy.

"So wet for me, aren't you, baby? Ready to be my good girl and take this cock in that pretty pussy?"

"Jax, please."

Without any further prompting, I line up my cock and push in barely two inches. My helmeted head falls back at the sensation of her pussy clenching around me. Pushing in another two inches, I grab her hips. There are still four more inches to go, and she's already panting with the delicious stretch of her pussy around my cock.

"Ready, baby?"

She nods her head, unable to form the words I so desperately want to hear. Grabbing a fistful of hair, I yank her head back, causing her back to arch.

"What have I told you about using your words, little sparrow?"

She looks back over her shoulder and smirks at me. "Yes, Jax, please... fuck me."

Keeping a grip on her hair, I slam into her tight pussy. She moans out at the delicious intrusion, pushing back onto my cock. My greedy little slut always wanting more...

I set a grueling pace, pulling out of her before slamming home. As my cock works her pussy, I reach a hand around and circle her clit. The added sensation soon has her tipping over the edge, and I feel her pussy clenching around my cock with her orgasm. One, two more thrusts and I'm falling with her, her name spilling from my lips.

We stay that way, both trying to catch our breath for a minute or two. When I pull out, I notice my cum leaking down her inner thigh. Before I even realize what I'm doing, I grab my cum with two fingers and shove it back inside her. Melody gasps at the feel of my fingers in her pussy, especially seeing that she's still sensitive from her orgasm.

She looks at me over her shoulder. "That was hot."

"Mmm," I growl back at her.

The motorcycle ride long forgotten, I fully take off my gear and hang it back up in the locker. Smacking her ass, we make our way to the elevator and up to the penthouse.

Grabbing Melody to me, I whisper in her ear, "Now it's my turn to lick your pretty pussy."

As the elevator dings, I smack her ass and she goes running for the bedroom. I stalk after her, the chase just adding even more fun to the mix.

As I gaze upon her in the bed, I can't help but to think that finally, everything is right in our world.

Melody is mine and I hers.

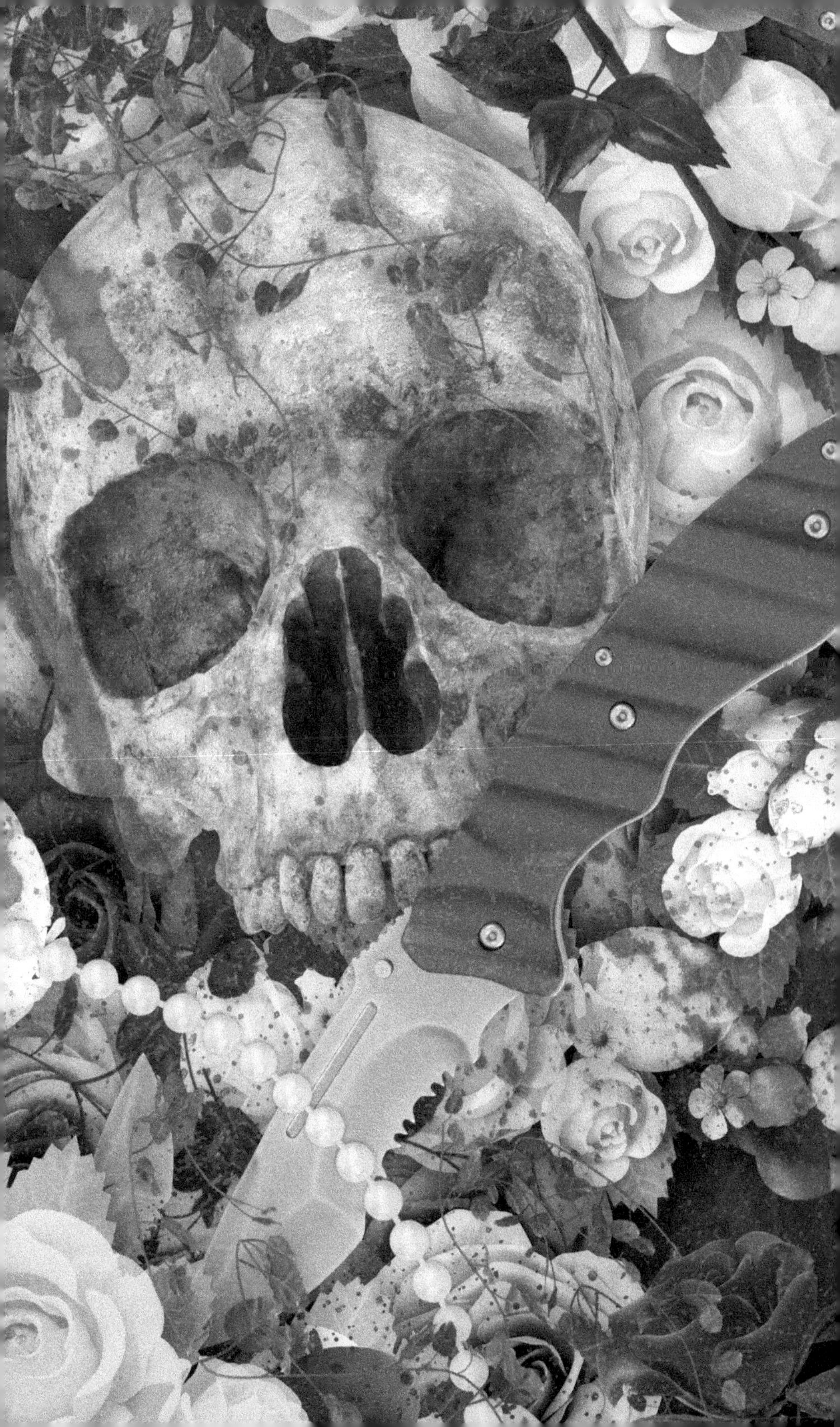

About the Author

Ashley McKnight is a debut author of contemporary dark romance. She loves to spend time with her husband and two children. When she isn't working full time, she enjoys reading and sharing her love of books and reading through her bookstagram.

If you'd like to follow Ashley McKnight on her author instagram, you can do so at the following link:

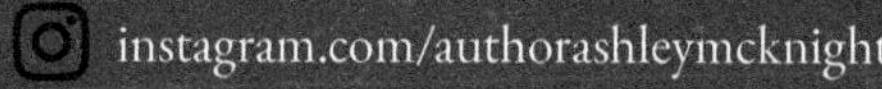

instagram.com/authorashleymcknight

Acknowledgments

I want to give thanks to the bookstagram community as it gave me the push and inspiration needed to finally write my own book. It was a dream of mine as a child that I just never gave much thought to as an adult. The booksta community inspired me to finally live my childhood dream and make it a reality.

A huge thank you to my beta readers: Rose, Dani, Victoria, Luanne, and Mariah and my editor Sadie. Without them I wouldn't have gotten this book polished to what it is now. They gave me critiqued suggestions and positive feedback that only helped and continues to help me to grow as an author. I am so appreciative of all their help in honing my book baby. Also, a special thanks to Rose and Dani, who helped with my dedication.

And to my husband for reading every chapter as I finished it, helping me rework certain scenes, and handling our kids so I had time to write, thank you. For pushing me when I went through a period of Imposter Syndrome, I couldn't have done any of this without your love and support.